Sunset Graze

Sunset Graze

LUKE SHORT

Thorndike Press • Thorndike, Maine

Library of Congress Cataloging in Publication Data:

Short, Luke, 1908-1975.
    Sunset graze / by Luke Short.
    p.   cm.
    Original ed. published by Doubleday, 1942.
    ISBN   0-89621-917-8 (alk. paper : lg. print)
    1. Large type books. I. Title.
[PS3513.L68158S86   1989]   89-33852
813'.54--dc20   CIP

Thorndike Press Large Print edition published in 1989 by
arrangement with H. N. Swanson, Inc.

Cover art by James B. Murray.

This book is printed on acid-free, high opacity paper.

Sunset Graze

CHAPTER 1

Across these two miles of sun-blasted desert the small black line faded and reappeared and faded again, but big Dave Wallace knew it was only the heat and that the stage was really coming. He sat down on his hot saddle again, his boots scuffing the thick gypsum dust of the wagon road as he did so, and closed his sore eyes. With the leaden stubbornness of a man to whom any movement has become a real effort of will, he eased the faded calico shirt from his baked back and considered that, for a man who was occasionally careless, he was also occasionally lucky.

Later, when the stage finally bore down on him, he was standing well away from his saddle, on which were his shell belt, bridle, saddle gun, and canteen. He did not want this mistaken for a holdup.

The stage driver had his look of assurance from a distance, and then the dry wail of his brakes lifted in the desert silence. The stage pulled up beside Dave, and for a moment he and the driver regarded each other in the white dust moiling up between them.

"You sure enough picked a spot," the driver observed.

"I wouldn't like to homestead it," Dave conceded.

"Tryin' to cut across from the Tanks and lost your horse, eh?"

Dave nodded rather than speak, for he had detected the near quiver in his voice when he spoke. The driver noticed it, too, and he looked sharply at Dave, seeing a big dusty man whose long sun-blackened face showed a hard and mighty patience. There was little else to remark about the man, save that behind squinted lids his eyes were an off shade of green-gray and his wide mouth oddly tight at the corners.

"Want a drink?"

"I got some left."

"Throw up your rig then."

Dave moved carefully as he handed up his rifle first. The barrel was so hot the driver cursed as he quickly laid it beside his shotgun on the seat. When Dave stooped to pick up his saddle there was a moment in which he paused to muster his strength. Then, lifting the saddle, he swung up on the wheel hub and heaved the saddle atop the stage.

"Ride inside," the driver said in a kindly voice. "It's dark in there."

8

Gratefully Dave stepped down. The dust curtains on the windows were anchored tightly, as well as the ones on the door. Courtesy made him peel off his flat-brimmed black Stetson and beat the dust from his half boots, his denim pants, and his shirt. Finished, he opened the stage door and climbed in. One brief glimpse of the dark interior showed him there was a woman in one seat, and he chose the opposite one as the stage rumbled into motion again.

As soon as he hit the seat Dave closed his eyes, and this time there was a blessed blackness behind his eyelids.

The woman opposite him felt on the seat beside her, and then leaned forward.

"Please," she said.

Dave did not answer.

She spoke louder. "Please, you're sitting on my hat."

Dave did not answer. Only then did the woman realize that he was already asleep, and she did not try to wake him.

The Dun River Range sprawled its timbered shoulders for three hundred miles in the shape of a rough crescent. Between the prongs of this crescent and stretching deep into the west was the desert. In the middle of the crescent, facing the desert and lying at its very edge against the great red sandstone cliffs from which it took its name, was the town of Vermillion. By day it

9

looked a little shabbier than the average cow town, because the great colored ramparts that boxed it in and dwarfed it were too gaudy in contrast. By night, however, Vermillion came into its rightful proportion, and Beth Hilliard, who had not seen it for two years, was glad the stage finished its journey after dark.

From the stage rolling down the single street she looked at the town. A few stores were still open, the light from their lamps laying a dim crossbarred square on the red dust of the street. Just as it was the night she had left, most of the ponies after dark were racked in front of the saloons. She noticed, with a slow smile of amusement at herself for doing so, that there was a new iron watering trough in front of Dugan's Monte Parlor.

Beyond the four corners the stage slowed and finally stopped rolling in front of Kissel's Feed Stable. Across from it the Vermillion Hotel with its gallery was only dimly lighted, but Beth could almost name the dozen loafers who were now sitting in their wired barrel chairs on the porch, feet on the rail.

When the driver opened the door she roused herself, stepped over the feet of the still-sleeping big man they had picked up on the desert, and descended. She was a tall girl, and even the two wearying days on the stage had not put a slack into her wide shoulders. The dust of the journey had dulled a little the sheen of her chestnut hair, which lay in a thick knot at the base of her neck, and it was the woman's instinct to arrive neat that made her take off her linen duster now.

The driver, helping her, asked, "Everything look the same, Miss Hilliard?"

"The same, only better, Curley."

She saw the three men descend the hotel steps, and without being able to see their faces in this dark she knew the one in the middle was Jess Gove. His high shoulders, his stately pace were the giveaway, and Beth advanced to meet him.

Jess Gove's hand was like leather, and when Beth took it and saw his smile she knew she was home. He was such a tall man that he was habitually hunched, as if to catch the words of lesser men below, and this, together with his thick ruff of dead-white hair, his slow, deliberate movements, gave the impression of a lesser god in half boots. Which was close enough to the truth for Beth, as it had been for her father.

"Now the sun can come up," old Jess said, and there was the same gentle teasing in his voice. "Beth, you been missed."

"So have you," Beth said, and they both smiled. "It's good to see you, Jess. You don't know how good."

"I know," Jess said. "I been back where they

11

grow corn and I can remember."

Jess turned now and called to the two men who had come out with him, but who, after touching their hats to Beth, had gone past her to the stage.

"Bring all the stuff up to the front room, boys."

Beth looked over and saw that they were unloading her luggage from the rear boot of the stage. Curley was on top, and he was handing down the saddle and rifle to the big man they had picked up on the desert.

Jess took her arm, and they headed for the hotel. Beth drew a deep breath into her lungs, sniffing the hot pungent odor of sun-baked rock that was Vermillion's own smell.

As they reached the boardwalk in front of the hotel steps one of the men at the stage called, "This green trunk come too, Miss Hilliard?"

Dave Wallace was halfway across the street when the man called. He halted, something clicking in his sleep-drugged mind at the sound of that voice. Without turning he slowly, fumblingly searched in his memory, not even hearing the girl's "Yes, please."

Now he had it. It came swiftly, shocking the sleep from him. He let the saddle slack off his shoulder into the dust, put his rifle on it, and walked back to the stage. There was a puncher in a faded blue shirt wrestling a trunk in the

12

rear boot. Below him, in the street, talking to him in a drawling tone of authority, was a tall, long-faced, bleach-eyed Texan.

Dave shouldered the Texan aside, reached up and grasped the shell belt of the man on the boot, and then he yanked. The man yelled and came over backward, and Dave broke his fall by kneeing his body. It flung the puncher on his hands and knees into the dust, and his hat rolled off. His face turned up to Dave, and for an instant there was blazing anger behind the surprise in it. Dave saw it was his man.

He reached down, balled up the man's shirt in his big hand, and yanked him up. When he was hip-high to him Dave drove his fist into the man's face with a down-beating, full-armed hook. The sound of the blow was clean in the night. The muffled thud of gristle-padded bone against flesh, and it was swift, vicious, instant. The man landed on his side, skidded two feet in a moil of red dust, and then rolled over on his face and was motionless.

There was one second of utter silence, and then the night was alive. Two punchers vaulted the porch railing of the hotel, their boots booming the boards of the walk as they landed and ducked under the tie rail on the run. A chair scraped the floor of the feed-stable office behind Dave, then crashed over as somebody ran out.

Dave heard and felt all this as he laid his glance on the tall Texan across from him, who stood staring stupidly, unbelievingly, from Dave to the downed man.

Now they were here, Dave saw — four punchers who came to a halt in front of him and behind him. They kept glancing over toward the hotel, and now Dave, curious, looked over too.

An overtall, stooped man left the girl and tramped deliberately toward him. In the half-light of the street Dave saw he wore a rusty black suit and half boots, the town clothes of a rancher. It was his face, though, that puzzled Dave. It was a kind face, the face of a patriarch, even to the thick jutting eyebrows which were as dead white as his hair.

He hauled up beside the downed man, looked briefly at him while the others alertly watched his face, and then he raised his glance to Dave.

"That sounded like a broken jaw," he said. His voice was mellow and tolerant.

"It was meant to be."

The older man studied him thoughtfully. "But why?"

"Ask him," Dave replied thinly.

The Texan man said quietly, "Better let us find out, Jess."

Dave's glance shuttled quickly to him. There

14

was a smug arrogance in the man's long face as he watched his boss. Dave knew instinctively that the Texan was used to this, that the crew was used to it, too, that they tolerated no challenge and refused no fight. He also knew that at a nod from the older man they would jump him, and the thought prodded a deep perversity in him.

"You can always try," he murmured.

The Texan didn't bother to look at him; he was watching Jess for the nod of assent. One of the punchers started cursing softly. Dave understood swiftly that he would have to crowd it hard to get out of here. He said to the older man, "If I see him again I'm apt to shoot him. Tell him that."

He turned and singled out one puncher and walked toward him, at him, as if he intended to walk him down. The puncher was a young man with a lean and reckless face. His hard, merry eyes took in immediately what Dave was doing, and he looked at the older man, not moving, begging for permission to start this.

There was a soft, flat, "No, Pete, no," from Jess, and then Pete stepped aside. Dave tramped on, as if he had not heard it, and when he reached his saddle he swung it to his shoulder and went on across the street toward the hotel. Behind him he heard a man swearing in passionate, toneless argument.

And then he was face to face with the girl of the stage, whom he recognized only by the color of her dress as she stood on the boardwalk.

He hauled up and touched his hat and said, "I'm sorry about that hat, miss. I didn't see it."

There was the tag end of fright in her face when he looked at her, and for a second she stared at him in open-eyed astonishment. In that moment Dave saw a kind of shocked gravity in her hazel eyes. It smoothed out the tired lines of her face, and Dave saw that she was young. Her mouth was full, her lips a little parted now, and her flatly molded cheekbones held a trace of color in them beneath the golden skin. Her ears were small, exposed by the manner of doing her hair, and he had a fleeting moment of pleasure at the way her hair swept back from her temple, flat and waving in small disarray.

The surprise was gone in a second, and it was followed by what Dave thought was confusion. It wasn't; it was resentment.

"It's all right," she said in a completely neutral voice. "It was just an old traveling hat."

Dave nodded and started for the steps. The girl's voice hauled him up.

"Why did you hit that man?"

Dave turned to look at her again and then said plainly, "Among other things, he's a liar."

16

"Do you know him?"

"No. I've talked with him."

"Then how do you know? He's worked for us for five years."

Dave said dryly. "Then you better get rid of him, miss," and again touched his hat and tramped up the steps into the hotel lobby. He was aware that the men on the porch had heard him and were watching him. He felt them watching during the long minutes in which he paid his dollar to the desk clerk, received his key, and slowly mounted the stairs.

In his room he threw his saddle in the corner and lighted the lamp, then stood there looking at it, a trace of a smile playing at the corners of his wide mouth. He felt a faint excitement still with him, but the murdering anger that had been in him for three days now was gone. Gingerly he put his fisted hand in the palm of his other hand and pressed. He grimaced a little, flexed his fingers, and then crossed the room and opened the door that led out onto the gallery.

He walked out onto the gallery and leaned both hands on the rail, looking down at the town. The street was empty of the crew. Across the way in front of the feed stable the hostler was hitching the fresh teams to the stage. On the boardwalk by the stage the soft-spoken Texan was talking to a woman. Idly Dave

17

watched as he assisted the woman into the stage, doffed his hat, and waited the few moments until the stage pulled out.

Dave turned back to his room, and there was an obscure feeling riding him that he was not going to like this town. Coming through the door, he scowled suddenly and blinked. His eyes, set wide-spaced in the deep wells under his heavy brows, were red-rimmed from the desert's glare and dust, and a kind of somber impatience fled across his face. There was a restlessness upon him as he glanced about the room at the paint-flaked iron bed, the chair, and the wash-stand.

Again he flexed his fingers, then, satisfied, stripped off his shirt. His flat back was pink where the desert sun had burned through his shirt. As he poured water into the basin the flat ropes of muscles across his shoulders moved gently under the skin. And then he was quiet, head cocked, listening.

He looked up now as he heard footsteps in the hall, and he watched the door. His glance dropped to the rifle in the corner and he waited, a big, still man who seemed as if he expected trouble.

The footsteps passed and he plunged his hands into the water. He was toweling his face and his thick black hair when he heard a knock on the door. Again his glance dropped to the

18

rifle in the corner as the knock was repeated, this time with peremptory firmness.

"All right," he said.

The door opened, and the Texan who had just put the woman on the stage sauntered in. Behind him, also entering, were two men, and one of them was the puncher Dave had hit. His shirt was tinted with the red dust of the street. The third man was a solid, thick-chested man in his middle thirties, and his movements were deliberate, almost ceremonial, as he stepped inside, closed the door behind him, and leaned against the wall. Two points of the star of the sheriff's office peeped out from under the V of his open vest. He seemed young, excessively sober.

"That him, Arnie?" the sheriff asked the Texan.

Arnie nodded. He came over and sat on the edge of Dave's bed, a lazy-seeming man with a quiet arrogance about him that he wore like his clothes. His bleached, bull-bold eyes were not even curious as he regarded Dave and then the room. A pale beard stubble accented the muscular lines of his face, and he was, Dave guessed, a man that had seldom known and never liked defeat.

The puncher Dave had hit stood sullenly between the other two, hands on hips, a smoldering dislike in his face which was already swelling into lopsidedness from Dave's blow.

Dave placed the towel carefully on the foot of the bed and picked up his shirt and said mildly to Arnie, "So you're still curious."

"Not me," the Texan drawled, not even looking at Dave.

"I am," the sheriff put in.

Dave tilted his head toward the puncher he had hit. "What does he say?"

The sheriff asked, "What do you, Ed?"

"I never seen him in my life."

Dave said calmly, "You're a purple liar."

It was as if they knew he would say this and didn't care. The man he had hit only looked away. The sheriff's expression of solemn gravity didn't change. Arnie, the real leader here, didn't seem to notice, and Dave thought swiftly, "He's done this before."

Arnie lifted a leg across his knee and held the ankle of his boot. With his other hand he prodded his Stetson off his forehead and ran his fingers through the hair on his temple several times, scratching. He yawned; he was bored.

The sheriff said to Dave, "What's your story then?"

Dave slipped into his shirt, and while buttoning it he considered carefully. He wouldn't be believed in what he said. On the other hand, he was curious and feeling a little reckless.

He said slowly, "Six days ago I rode in on a

20

horse camp by the last water hole over in the Mesquite Hills – his camp." He nodded to the puncher he had hit. "I was headed across the desert for Vermillion and I asked about the water at the Bunchgrass Tanks. He said he'd come across three days ago and the Tanks were full." He paused. "They weren't."

"Not this time of year," the sheriff said.

Dave said dryly, "I can tell you that now."

"What happened?"

"I lost a good horse and a pack horse," Dave murmured, watching the puncher. "I got pretty hot too."

Arnie drawled indifferently, "You got a poor memory for faces. Ed wasn't there."

Dave smiled, still looking at the puncher. "I know. He was with you, wasn't he?"

Then he looked at Arnie, who was watching him carefully. For five full seconds Arnie regarded him, and Dave saw the slow controlled anger mount in his eyes. "That's right," Arnie murmured.

"Sure," Dave jeered softly.

There was a moment of uneasy silence, and then the sheriff said in rising protest, "That's not a nice thing to accuse a man of. I happen to know you're wrong."

"Sure you do."

The sheriff was vaguely aware of the irony in Dave's voice, and his protest continued: "Why would a man send you out on the desert to a dry water hole? For a ragging? I don't believe it."

"It wasn't for a ragging," Dave murmured. His attention was on the puncher now, and he saw the man's face smooth out, saw him brace himself for what was coming. "I just asked him a question."

Dave could feel the tension in the room. Arnie was utterly still on the bed. Only the sheriff seemed puzzled, unaware of what Dave was saying.

"What question?" the sheriff asked.

"How Tip Macy really died."

The sheriff's face showed only bafflement. Dave judged him a man who tried to add onto his years and hide a slow-wittedness behind the deliberateness of manner. He was sure of it when the sheriff said protestingly, "Macy died in a blizzard. We had a bad winter here."

Dave said nothing. Slowly, then, it came to the sheriff that something was not right here. His bafflement made him frown; he turned his stubborn face to Arnie. "I don't get it."

Arnie drawled idly, almost contemptuously, "He claims Ed sent him on to the Bunchgrass Tanks because he asked about Tip Macy."

"But Tip Macy died in a storm."

Arnie nodded toward Dave and said patiently, "He don't believe it."

"How did he die?" the sheriff asked Dave. "That's what I'd like to find out."

Both Arnie and the sheriff looked at Dave. Arnie, then, rose lazily and drawled, "That's what the ruckus was about, Kinsley. He made a mistake. Ed was with me." He paused. "You want us any more?"

"No," Sheriff Kinsley said in a stubborn, grim voice. "No, go on."

Arnie and Ed went out. When they were gone Sheriff Kinsley folded his arms and said flatly, "Tip Macy worked for Chevron, the Dun River Cattle Company. That was Arnie Chance, their foreman, and Ed Seegrist, a Chevron hand. Tip Macy was caught in a blizzard up in the high country this winter and buried there, because the snow was so deep we couldn't get to him. His death was reported to me, and I certified it." His voice was growing hard. "Now, either you're crazy, or a damned trouble-maker. Which are you?"

"You been handed some taffy, Sheriff," Dave murmured.

Sheriff Kinsley pushed away from the wall. A slow flush worked up into his broad face, making it stubborn, making the dark eyes hard and angry.

"I'm being handed some right now," Kinsley said.

"No. I want to make a suggestion."

23

"So do I. I suggest you go back where you came from. Starting tomorrow."

Dave didn't reply.

"There's a stage west out of here tomorrow. You be on it."

Kinsley wheeled and tramped out of the room, slamming the door behind him. Dave stared at the door a moment, the caution dying from his face, his eyes almost musing. He was thinking that he had found all the proof he needed tonight. It would never hold up in any court, but then it was not meant to. It lay in Ed Seegrist's face, in the elaborate but watchful indifference that Arnie Chance had shown him.

His memory fled back to that winter afternoon in the barroom of a way-station town some six hundred miles from here. The steady snow outside had kept the crews from the neighboring ranches at home. He was waiting in the warm and almost deserted saloon while the blacksmith downstreet replaced a broken felloe in the wagon wheel he had left. There was a drink in front of him, and he was leafing through the stack of newspapers on the bar when he saw the item. It was in the weekly newspaper printed on the Ute reservation over on the Dun River Range. It said: *Cattlemen are suffering heavy losses in the constant blizzards that are sweeping this country. A grim note was added to these tales of suffering when it was*

24

learned that Tip Macy, well known on the reservation here as an employee of the Dun River Cattle Co., was found frozen to death after the blizzard of 19th inst. Macy, a plains-country man and unaware of the ferocity of our blizzards, apparently was set afoot by his horse and after several hours of wandering without sufficient clothes succumbed to exposure. He had read it three times and rejected this information, as men do who instinctively refuse to believe a friend is dead. He had written to Tip Macy that afternoon with paper and pencil borrowed from the bartender. In the weeks that passed he received no answer from Tip, nor, what was stranger, Tip's wife. And then in the slow winter months when a man had the leisure to think he had arrived at the decision that something was wrong. He founded his belief on two things — Tip Macy was not a plains-country man, for Dave had spent two winters with him in that hell of the Montana high country. When the winter was over and spring came, with its restlessness, he left to find out about Tip Macy. And now he thought he knew. His hunch was right.

Now Dave looked at his gun belt a still moment and then ignoring it, picked up his Stetson and went out. On Vermillion's street there was a brooding stillness broken only by the piano in one of the downstreet saloons.

Dave felt the night heat and did not know that it was the great rearing sandstone walls behind the town that stored up the day's heat to release it at night.

When he saw a restaurant that was still open he stepped inside. There was a girl behind the counter, talking to a man, and when they both looked up Dave saw the puncher was the same one he had almost walked down by the stage. The tall man had called him Pete.

The waitress came toward him, and for a moment Dave had a moment of doubt. She'd repeat his question to Pete, who would repeat it to his boss. Still, they knew why he was here, and it was too late to cover up now.

"I'm looking for a Mrs. Macy — Martha Macy," Dave said to the girl. "Where can I find her?"

The girl pointed across the street. "She lives with another girl above the saddle shop. That's across from the saloon."

Dave thanked her and, turning full around, saw Pete between him and the door. Pete was standing there with a brash grin on his face, his eyes full of hell, his hat pushed back on his forehead, revealing short, unruly pale hair.

There was something tough and likeable about him as he stood there and said to Dave, "This time you walk around me."

Dave regarded him a moment and then

smiled. "That's fair enough," he said, and he walked around him and stepped out into the night, still smiling.

A lone pony tied in front of the restaurant whickered, and looked longingly at the cluster of horses in front of the saloon three doors away. Then he looked at Dave, mildly begging, and thrust his nose out to sniff at Dave's shirt.

Dave patted him and swung under the tie rail, heading for the saddle shop. This was not an hour to ask questions, but it had to be done. The sheriff's order was there for him to accept or reject, and Dave had given it no thought. But if he stayed he knew it would be harder to see Tip Macy's wife tomorrow than it was now.

An outside staircase let onto a landing at the second story of the building. Dave climbed it and knocked loudly on the door. When his knock was not answered he repeated it. Almost immediately, under his hand, the door was opened a crack.

"I'm looking for Mrs. Macy," Dave said, touching his hat.

A woman's irritable voice said, "She's not here any more."

Dave, sensing the hostility in her voice, thrust his foot in the door crack. "Where is she?"

"She's gone. She's left town. Now go away!"

"Where did she go?"

27

"I don't know," the woman said bitingly. "She's not the kind to go out with you cowboys at night, and you ought to know that. Now go away!"

Dave withdrew his foot, and the door was slammed and swiftly locked.

He came down the steps, baffled and a little angry. He hadn't come six hundred miles to be put off with this vague explanation.

On the boardwalk below he stood hesitant and then turned downstreet.

At the feed stable there was a lantern hanging on a nail in the archway. The office was lighted but empty. Dave tramped down the runway to the corral in back and found nobody and came up to it again, pausing in the doorway.

Presently a man cut across from Dugan's Monte Parlor. He hurried a little when he saw the customer in the doorway.

When Dave put his question the old man rubbed his face and looked out into the night, the smell of liquor redolent on his breath.

"Mrs. Macy. Yes, I know her."

"Did she take a stage out of here?"

"That's right. For Hilliard."

"When was that?"

The old man looked at him, surprised, and said, "Why, tonight. The one you come in on. Wasn't that what you was talkin' about?"

CHAPTER 2

Beth Hilliard had barely cleaned the dust of travel from herself when there was a knock on her door. She opened it and saw Sam Kinsley, hat in hand, standing beside Jess Gove and smiling.

"Hello, Sam," Beth said, pleasure in her voice. She shook hands with him, and Kinsley's square face was flushed with pleasure.

"Come in for a while," Beth invited.

"No," Sam said hastily. "You're tired, and I've got work to do. I'll go on. I just wanted to say hello to you, Beth. You're looking fine."

"You too, Sam," Beth said. "You aren't very fierce-looking for a sheriff," she added slyly, laughing.

"I'm not a very fierce sheriff," Kinsley said. He passed a few more words with her, and then Beth said, "Would you mind if I kept Jess?"

Kinsley said he wouldn't, said good night, and left, and Jess stepped into the room, saying, "Why not wait until you're rested, Beth?"

"I couldn't," Beth said. "I've been waiting for weeks, Jess."

She closed the door after him. Her luggage was piled on the floor at the foot of the bed, and Jess walked around it, taking the straight chair by the wall.

He sat down, sighing, and Beth said, "It's nice to see Sam. Is he a good sheriff, Jess?"

"None better," Jess said. He looked around for a place to put his hat, and then compromised by putting it on the floor.

Beth said, "Do you want to send down for cigars or a drink, Jess?"

"No," Jess drawled. "You don't want me to, either. All you want is to hear what I've got to say."

Beth's face was suddenly grave, and she nodded. "I guess that's it, Jess. Since I got your letter telling me I'd better come out I've imagined a thousand things. The worst news couldn't be as bad as I've imagined."

Jess hitched his chair sideways under him and leaned an arm across the back of it. There was a close, searching interest in his face as he regarded her while she came to the bed and sat down.

"Beth," he said, "do you want it now, all at once, the whole thing?"

"You know I do, Jess."

"All right," Jess said. "You're broke. You're as

flat broke as I am. Last summer you were a rich girl. You aren't now. Your two-thirds share in the Dun River Cattle Company is worth thirty head of winter-starved cattle, part of three or four shacks, a heap of letter paper with our name on it, and two-thirds right to an Indian-grass lease that's got the grass money due on it in a month or so."

"Oh, Jess," Beth whispered. She was silent a long moment, her lips parted in a kind of breathless attention. "Is that true?"

"I'm afraid it is."

Beth's glance fell then, and she sat motionless on the bed, save for the small movement of her hands pleating and unpleating a fold of her blue dress. The lamp on the table beside her bed started to smoke, and she rose now and turned down the wick. Then she looked again at Jess Gove, and she saw the dismal sympathy in his face.

She laughed shortly now. "That sort of took my breath away, Jess. I — somehow, I'd imagined everything but that."

"I was kind of rough," Jess said. "Anyway, you know now."

"What happened, Jess?"

"The worst winter a man ever knew," Jess said grimly. "Fall blizzards, sleet, thaws, cold, thaws, rain, and blizzard piled on top of blizzard. The cattle just gave up,

Beth. So did the crew."

"What was our loss?"

Jess shook his head tiredly. "You wouldn't believe it, girl. Over ninety per cent. On two thousand head."

Beth rose now and walked around the bed to the gallery door. She opened it, and then her hand remained on the knob, during a long moment of abstraction. She glanced at Jess then and sighed softly.

"That's the way the best things end, I guess." She walked back to the foot of the bed and stood there, regarding the older man, and there was a wry smile on her face. "Poor Dad. I think this is the only time I've been glad he isn't alive. I don't think he could have taken this, Jess."

"He could take anything."

"Yes, but I'm glad he didn't have to hear this." A softness came into her face now; her mouth turned up a little at the corners. "When I think of the one-room shacks Mother kept house in and the way Dad used to save his cigar money and the hand-me-downs I used to wear, I'm glad Dad isn't here to know this, Jess. It — well, it just wouldn't be right to have slaved and sacrificed half a lifetime for something you want, and then see it all go in one winter."

Her smile was soft now, made so by memory. "Do you remember, Jess, the day Dad paid the first grass money to the Utes?"

"I remember," Jess said gently.

"He came home so drunk Mother had to put him to bed. She just looked at him sleeping there and smiled and said, 'I hope he got drunk for both of us.'"

Jess nodded. Beth took a deep breath now and slowly walked around and sat on the bed, facing Jess.

"What about you, Jess? If I am broke, you're broker."

"I'm too old to care much, Beth," Jess said simply. He made a loose gesture of impatience, with his hand. "I keep waking up at night and wondering if I could have helped it."

"Nobody can help winter."

"But you didn't see what I did," Jess said gloomily. "Those two thousand head of Texas steers started the winter on our lease on the reservation. After the first three blizzards they were scattered from hell to breakfast all over the slope. A band of them traveled sixty miles to die in a cut of the North Fork. Their bodies were stacked forty feet high there, Beth, and when the snow went off they backed up the waters in the creek for a mile. All over it was like that."

"It must have been terrible," Beth agreed softly. It was probably a combination of this news and the days of traveling, but she felt

33

weary and discouraged, and she wanted solitude to adjust herself to this new situation. She fought down the feeling and straightened her back and said matter-of-factly, "What's left, Jess?"

"Nothing. I mean that, too. Nothing."

"But there's our lease with the Utes. We have a hundred thousand acres of reservation grass leased. Surely we can sell our right to lease Indian grass to other cattlemen."

Jess shook his head. "Have you forgot the terms of that lease, Beth? It's not worth a dollar to anybody but us."

"But why, Jess?"

"Your Dad and me got the first lease from the Indians. They liked us, and we were square with them. You remember what we pay them?"

"A cent an acre, isn't it?"

Jess nodded. "But other cattlemen are paying two and two and a half cents an acre for grass not as good as ours. We got a bargain, Beth, but by the terms of the lease we can't transfer it. As long as Joe Hilliard's heirs or me or my heirs lease that grass the rent is a cent an acre. But when the lease day comes around that we can't pay, then our lease reverts back to the Utes again." He paused. "You see what that means, girl?"

"Not quite, Jess?"

"It means no bank or no cattlemen will loan

us money to lease or to stock the lease. Because if we can't pay the Indians, then our lease is thrown open to the highest bidder. And they want that grass for themselves. They'd be fools to loan us money," he finished bitterly.

"But haven't we friends, Jess?"

"Who?"

Beth shook her head. "I don't know. But Dad helped so many people, and you have too."

Jess shook his head. "I've tried to borrow, Beth. I've swallowed my pride and I've begged, but it didn't work." He added gently, with no rancor in his voice, "Folks have got a short memory when remembering will cost them something. No, we can't borrow."

Beth sat up now. "So we're cleaned out, Jess?"

Jess nodded.

"What do you want me to do?"

Jess picked up his hat and came to his feet. "Just try not to think about it," he said. He looked at her now, his face sad, his expression gentle. "Tomorrow, Beth, I want to talk over a scheme with you. It may give you a little money — very little money. I want you to talk it over with Sam and me in the morning."

"What is it, Jess? I want to know."

"No. Tomorrow, Beth. We'll see Sam in the morning, and then I'll tell you."

At that moment he looked so tired and beaten

that Beth felt the stronger. She slipped her arm through his and went to the door with him.

Jess opened it and looked down at her and smiled and shook his head. "It was pretty rough, wasn't it, Beth? I'm sorry it had to be that way."

"Maybe tomorrow it won't look so bad."

"Maybe. Good night, Beth."

"Good night, Jess."

Beth closed the door behind him and came back into the middle of the room. What it boiled down to, she thought bitterly, was that she had come to bury her father's dream. The years of sacrifice, the endless notes at the bank, the slow progress, the hard, comforting knowledge that time would win for them — all this had been lost in this short winter. Again she thought of old Jess Gove, wise and quiet and not wanting more than any simple man wanted, and it made her sad. The ranked luggage on the floor was a symbol of this defeat now. She had come home to nothing. She walked around it toward the open gallery door, remembering the packing, the homesickness for this country, the wanting to get back despite the bad news she had read between the lines in Jess's letter.

She stepped out onto the gallery from the lamplit room and walked over to the gallery rail, and she was wondering what Jess's scheme of tomorrow would be. Vermillion's street was deserted, and as her eyes slowly adjusted themselves to the dark she was aware that someone else was out here. Turning her head, she saw a man leaning against a gallery post. The smell of cigarette smoke came to her, and then she recognized the man in the stage.

She felt him looking at her and didn't know what to say, and yet she wouldn't be driven back to her room because of his presence.

Below, Jess Gove tramped down the hotel steps and cut across the street. Beth knew he was on his way to Dugan's Monte Parlor for a nightcap that he never missed when he was in town.

And then the man spoke quietly. "You know that man, miss?"

"Since I can remember."

"You trust him, too?"

The bland, bald effrontery of the question brought a quick retort from Beth. "Like I would my father."

"I wonder why," the man murmured.

His cigarette arced out into the street, and he was in his room before Beth could unravel an answer from the anger that was in her.

CHAPTER 3

A sound night's sleep put a thin whistle on
Dave Wallace's lips this morning. He stepped
out of his room, ravenous for breakfast, and saw
a puncher standing at the end of the corridor,
back to him, idly looking out the window. Dave
hardly remembered him. As he went down the
steps into the lobby the sharp smell of bacon
and coffee came to him with a savage goodness
about it. Cutting through the lobby, he entered
the dining room. A waitress who had been
talking to a lone puncher brought him some
coffee and later a huge breakfast, which he
wolfed down with hungry concentration.

Afterward he paid his check and walked out
to the lobby street door, rolling a cigarette on
the way. He paused in the doorway, touching a
match to his cigarette and looked out upon the
town. This was its most pleasant hour, when
the steep cliffs had cooled off and now walled
out the sun, and the street was surprisingly
busy.

Dave admired the close cliffs briefly, then,

drawing the smoke deep into his lungs, he looked around him. The first thing he saw then was the lanky, indolent body of Arnie Chance lounged in one of the porch chairs. The events of last night which had been shouldered out of his mind by the simple fact of hunger now returned, and once more he was reminded of what was going to happen. He considered Chance for a full moment, studying the man's long profile, recalling his careless arrogance of last night. He dropped his smoke, which didn't taste so good now, and carefully ground it beneath his heel.

A careful pessimism was on him now and made him turn to survey the lobby. The puncher he had seen in the corridor above was now sitting on the bottom step of the stairs engrossed in rolling a smoke, and Dave recognized him as the man he had almost walked down last night. There was another puncher talking to the desk clerk, and this was the man who had been in the dining room, and one of the Chevron hands too.

It was a game now. Dave looked across the street, noting the stage which was making up, and he saw a puncher idling by the feed-stable door. And down the street under the wooden awning of a store Ed Seegrist was backed against a building front. A hard impersonal admiration for Arnie Chance came to Dave, and he stepped out and paused by the porch post, looking at Chance.

Presently Chance turned his head, and they looked at each other a moment.

"A beautiful morning," Dave murmured.

"For traveling," Chance drawled.

"I think I'll like this country," Dave said blandly. "I think I'll stick."

Chance didn't even smile, and Dave went down the steps and turned downstreet. He knew what was going to happen; he wanted to crowd it, to see how it would happen.

He was beyond Chance on the empty boardwalk and had passed the corner of the hotel porch when Sheriff Kinsley stepped out, as if by accident, from the door of the store next door. Dave slowed his pace, and for a moment there was a wild impulse in him to break for it, to watch the fun of the hunt. Only he knew he wouldn't do it.

The sheriff was wearing a gun belt this morning. There was something solid and implacable about him as he placed his stocky body in the middle of the boardwalk and waited for Dave to approach. There was something careful, wary, iron-willed in Kinsley's square face, too, as Dave stepped aside to let a woman pass him, then came to a halt in front of Kinsley.

"You haven't much time," Kinsley

observed meagerly.

Dave didn't answer, only turned and looked backstreet. Chance had come out of his chair and stood by the rail, quietly watching this. Beyond him a Chevron puncher waited on the boardwalk, also attentive.

"All your deputies?" Dave inquired.

"Friends."

"The kind that are always willing to do you a favor, aren't they?" Dave murmured.

Kinsley's sober face didn't alter. He was the sort of a man, Dave thought, who was impervious to prodding, a kind of slow, dogged man who would be hard to anger and a fanatical fighter when he was roused. Kinsley raised a hand, pointed a thick, blunt finger, and said quietly, "There's your stage."

Dave nodded.

He turned back, angling across the street. Now he saw a puncher bringing his saddle, bridle, and rifle to the stage, and he had another moment of grudging pleasure at the thoroughness with which this was being done.

The others, Chance and the sheriff and Seegrist and two more men, converged on the stage now. A drummer and a ranch wife, who had been waiting by the office door, now climbed into the stage, and the driver slammed the door.

Dave swung up into the stage seat. The

41

driver, from his side, climbed up and then halted on the wheel hub when he saw Dave, a look of puzzlement in his face.

"George."

It was Arnie Chance's drawl, and the driver turned and looked down. Chance, with his unconscious insolence, flipped a coin in the air, and the driver reached out with his free hand and caught it and looked at it.

"Put him off at Five Troughs."

Five of them were down there, all studying Dave with an expression of faint amusement on their faces. The driver held the coin tentatively, still standing on the hub, and then said to the sheriff, "That right, Kinsley?"

"That's right."

The driver climbed up, seated himself, unwound the ribbons from the brake arm, and Dave looked down at Arnie Chance.

"You owe me two horses, friend – a pack horse and a saddle horse," he murmured. "I'll be back to collect."

For the first time Arnie Chance smiled. It was a slow, taciturn smile, stemming from deep amusement.

"Help yourself," he drawled. "The company brand's a Chevron. Just don't get caught, that's all."

The driver kicked off the brake and the stage started rolling. Dave relaxed now, his body

42

slacking easily with the lurching of the stage, and he watched the last stores and then the shacks of Vermillion thin out onto the edge of the desert. The tawny, shimmering reaches of it lay ahead, drinking in the mounting sun. Dave knew suddenly that he was not going to cross it.

But first there were some things he wanted to know, and he pondered them briefly. The man they called Jess, the tall kindly man with the mild voice, was the boss of these men. He owned Arnie Chance, and Chance ruled the others, and they were men ready to fight. The girl whose name he didn't know he couldn't peg. A man had only to look at her to know she didn't understand this crew. A woman could watch something like what happened last night and see nothing that lay beneath it. Yet she had told him that she trusted the old man they called Jess.

Dave asked idly of the driver, "Who owns this Dun River Cattle Company?"

The driver, who was younger than yesterday's driver, looked obliquely at him and turned his suspicion to Dave's question. Dave gave him time, knowing the man was wary of him because of Chance's orders, knowing, too, that he must search for the harm that would lie in his answer.

Finally, he answered, "Jess Gove owns some

of it. Beth Hilliard, Joe Hilliard's daughter, owns the most."

Dave said, "She come home yesterday on the stage, didn't she?"

"That's right."

Dave thought of her now, and oddly he remembered her hair. It was a chestnut color, like the color of the true chestnut horse, and there was a streak of lighter hair through it. It started on the right side of her forehead and lay silvery and plain for a man to see in a certain light, as he had seen it on the gallery last night. He knew surely that Beth Hilliard had never questioned how Tip Macy had died, would not think it strange that Martha Macy had been put on the stage for Hilliard after he arrived. He had one more question.

"Hilliard? Haven't I heard of a town named that?"

"It's back in the mountains," the driver said. "It was named for Joe Hilliard. It's headquarters for Chevron, for the company."

Afterward Dave was patient. He studied the stage teams now, noting the quality of each horse, finally settling his favor on a short-coupled black who was the off leader. He smoked two cigarettes and looked indifferently at the desert, which he did not like.

Presently, judging it was time, his glance fell to the shotgun, its butt in the boot, its barrel leaning against the driver's leg. Reaching over for it, he lifted it by the barrel and flung it overboard. Before the surprise was fully in the driver's face Dave pulled his own gun and held it loosely on his lap in his right hand.

His left arm circled the driver and got his six-gun, which also went overboard.

The driver started to pull up, and Dave said, "Go on a ways."

The driver kept looking at Dave's gun, and once he looked up and said, "The only money I got is what Arnie Chance give me."

"Pull up," Dave said.

The stage came to a stop, and the driver kicked the brake on.

"Get down," Dave ordered.

Surlily, a little frightened, too, the driver swung down. Dave climbed back, threw his saddle and bridle down to the driver, and then said, "Cut out the black in the lead and put my saddle on to him."

At that moment the stage door opened and the drummer put his foot out on the step and looked up, squinting at Dave.

Dave leveled his gun at the man and said, "Get back in there and stay there."

The drummer vanished like a trap-door spider, and Dave hunkered comfortably down on the stage top.

"Take your time," he drawled to the driver. "I

got all day, and so have you."

The first edge had been worn off the stage horses, so that the black submitted docilely but curiously to the saddling. Dave could tell from the way the horse acted that it had been ridden before but only barely.

When the driver was finished Dave ordered him to cut out the other lead horse, tie him to the rear boot, and stow the harness.

When that was done Dave stepped down, carrying his rifle, and took the reins of the black from the driver.

"Get going," he said. "Don't turn back for your guns. I'll be on the road, so I'll know."

He stood there until the driver had whipped his four horses into motion again and was a good way off.

Slipping his rifle into the saddle scabbard, he tightened his shell belt, lifted his six-gun from its holster, and rammed it tightly in the waistband of his pants, and then put a foot in the stirrup. This was a strange horse, a half-broken horse, and Dave was careful.

His next move was a lightning-fast attempt to get a leg over and a foot in the off stirrup, at which he only partially succeeded. The half-broken black was alert enough to come unlocked immediately, and for a long minute he tried desperately to unseat Dave. Presently he gave up; Dave reined him around, checking a

46

small nosebleed with his free hand, and put him into a walk.

He was headed for the Dun River Range, which sloped brown and green-black up to the snowy reaches of the peaks.

CHAPTER 4

Old Ives dropped down into Hilliard about nine this night, and when his mare crossed the rough bridge that spanned the Little Dun she seemed to step softly, as if she had learned to copy old Ives's quiet ways. The town itself lay on the flat in the bend of the river and hardly deserved to be called a town. Planted as it was in the widened cleft of a deep canyon in the timbered reaches of the Dun River Range, it could boast of a bare dozen buildings fronting each other across a narrow rutted street. The buildings one side of the street were backed against the slope, and when a boulder broke loose from the rimrock above, as it occasionally did, it came to rest in the back rooms of these buildings. The buildings south of the street teetered on the edge of the river, and from this direction a man had to go through the whole town to reach the stable and corral, built on the wildest spot in town.

Privately old Ives considered the rain- and sun-bleached frame buildings of Hilliard a tick on the fair body of the mountain range he loved, and only necessity drew him here tonight.

The porch of the hotel was just level with a mounted man's head, and it was the first building after crossing the bridge. Ives didn't look at it, the thought of having to sleep in one of its beds already making him uncomfortable.

He passed the Olympus Saloon farther down the riverside of the street and without having to look knew the brands of most of the ponies tied there, and among them would be Chevron. This was Chevron's town, founded by Joe Hilliard who, like Ives himself, so hated the desert that he couldn't abide Vermillion.

Ives put his horse in the corral downstreet and walked up the road in the dark, heading for the saloon.

He was an old man, small, wiry, and he moved down the rutted street as noiseless as smoke, his moccasins barely whispering as he moved. In front of the Olympus he paused among the horses tied there, stroking them absently, looking past the lower half of the windows, which were painted an opaque and peeling white, into the saloon.

The horses nuzzled at his tattered pants and buckskin shirt, both of which smelled of wood smoke, and old Ives spoke to them affectionately while he had his look. There was a spring chill in the night's air, but Ives's shirt was open. He wore no hat, and the hair shearing which he bought once a year in the spring was only weeks old. The long clean lines of his skull were not yet hidden by the quarter-inch fuzz of pepper-and-salt hair that was as stiff and thick as a wire brush.

Having had his look, he snorted softly, ducked under the hitch racks, and shouldered through the doors of the Olympus. The saloon was a medium-sized room, well lighted by three overhead kerosene lamps. A big barrel stove, its pipe shafting straight to the ceiling, stood in its sanded box halfway down the room. The rear half of the saloon held three big tables flanked with heavy chairs, and the walls there were lined with the pictures cut from distillery calendars so old some of them were brown and curling.

The smell of tobacco smoke and beer slops and whiskey affronted old Ives's nostrils as he walked up to the bar on the right.

It was a puncher playing poker at one of the rear tables who first saw Ives and whooped, "Here's the wolfer!"

There were perhaps a dozen men in the saloon, and every one of them called a greeting to Ives, grinning with pleasure and winking at each other.

Old Ives moved down the bar, shaking hands

ceremoniously with three of the Chevron crew, two of them Ed Seegrist and Pete Framm, and then moved back to the tables, where the games were abandoned to greet him.

"Even the bears beat you out this spring, Ives," one of the punchers said.

"I never been holed up," Ives said scornfully, and added with full sarcasm, "Not like some I know." To the bartender he called carelessly, "Set up the house."

The men collected around him now, smiling, talking, and Ives answered their questions patiently. This was a kind of ceremony, celebrating his first appearance in Hilliard since winter.

"The deer up as far as Peak Lake, yet, Ives?"

Ives regarded his questioner, and the men started to grin. "You think I'd tell a damn butcher like you if they was?" Ives asked sourly.

This was a joke among them, the fatherly way Ives protected the game here, lying as to its whereabouts, never missing an opportunity to hand out misinformation.

"Make any money this winter, old-timer?" Ed Seegrist asked.

Ives said sourly, "Three times as much as you did."

"You ain't been to collect bounty from us yet?"

"I'll take four hundred dollars from Chevron,"

51

Ives said calmly. "That is, unless Jess changed his mind about payin' twenty dollars for grays."

The men whistled, and old Ives looked obscurely pleased. Without Ives as a contrast, these men looked work-hardened and weather-browned. Alongside him they looked almost soft and pale. His skin had reached the color and texture where weather could do no more to it. His pale eyes were as alert and content as an animal's, and there was a simple grace and economy about his movements that was almost Indian. Joe Hilliard had found him ten years ago, a fiddle-footed squaw-man trapper, and had hired him to keep down the gray wolves that preyed on his stock. He had become an institution on the Dun River Range; no ranch house, no line camp, no Indian lodge was stranger to him. He knew every creek and canyon of this range; more, he knew its men and its politics and its hates and greeds, and he never talked, fending off the curious with a taciturn hostility or a savage ill-humor that was his defense. He had two friends. One had been Joe Hilliard; tonight he was seeing the other.

The drinks came, and Ives waited a decent interval and then asked the bartender, "Where's Con?"

The bartender nodded toward the door in the side wall at the head of the bar. "In the office."

Ives pulled out from the crowded bar

and went up to the door and opened it without knocking.

He shut it behind him and was in a tiny office barely big enough to hold the two chairs, the roll-top desk, and the great mountain of flesh seated at it, back to the door.

"It's about time you drifted in," Con Buckley said without turning.

"How the hell did you know?"

"Moccasins," Con said. "It's you or an Indian. Any Ute comes in here without knocking gets kicked right through that wall, and they know it."

Con swung his chair around and regarded Ives with a dry, pleased affection. Con Buckley was a bald Irishman with features that sat oddly with the rest of him. His face was small, delicate, with a tiny hooked nose and pouting lips that were almost obliterated by the great jowls of the man. His body was huge, formless, his neck lost in the great mantle of flesh on his shoulders. When he sat his thick thighs pushed his legs apart, and his belly always kept him a foot from the desk. His body was monstrous, but old Ives, who hated freaks of nature, had gone beyond that, past the dead, cynical eyes, into the heart of the man, and had found him wise, tough, and just.

Con took a bottle of Irish whisky from a bottom drawer of the desk and set two glasses beside it on the desk.

"That," old Ives said surlily, nodding toward the bottle, "is why I don't come oftener."

"Nevertheless, you'll have a drink with me."

Ives took the drink Con offered him and sat in the other chair. The murmur of voices through the thin partition was a plain, almost comfortable sound.

Con said, "Have a good winter?"

"I made money."

"Who cares about that? You don't."

Ives shook his head. "Winters ain't what they used to be for me now Joe's dead."

"You missed Christmas at the Chevron?"

Ives nodded. Con studied him thoughtfully, and then his glance was veiled a little. "Why?" he asked quietly.

"Jess Gove."

"A fine man," Con said.

"And you're a liar," Ives said placidly.

"The kindest, softest-spoken, biggest-hearted man this country ever saw. Why, you only got to look at him to see that." There was no inflection in Con's voice, no expression on his face.

Ives said nothing.

Con asked, "You don't believe it?"

"No."

"Tell me what I said that was wrong."

Ives thought a minute. "Nothin'. Only

54

that ain't the man."

Con sighed. "That's what I think. Damned if I know why it ain't, though." He drank his whisky, smacking his lips over it. Ives drank his, too, and his expression of perplexity deepened. He shifted in his chair, and when he spoke his voice was low, earnest.

"Con, I've known you some time. I'm goin' to tell you a couple of things and then ask you some questions."

Con was silent, watching him, and Ives went on, "If you don't want to answer them, say so."

"Ask your questions."

Ives thought a minute. "I've heard from three-four outfits that Chevron was cleaned out this winter."

Con nodded.

"A big winterkill," Ives went on. "All right, I been travelin' since the snow went off. I've covered a lot of ground, more than any Chevron steer would cover in a winter. I saw dead cattle, a lot of 'em." He paused, wishing to isolate what he was going to say now. "Trouble was, damn few of 'em was Chevron."

Con rubbed a fat leg with the palm of his hand waiting.

"Where'd they die, then?" Ives asked.

Con said, "What's the other question?"

"This'll hurt," Ives said.

"Go on."

55

"Joe Hilliard set you up here," Ives said bluntly. "Somethin's happenin'. You might not know what it is, but you know Jess Gove ain't the man Joe Hilliard thought he was. His crew is gettin' tough. Arnie Chance ain't a bucko top hand any more; he's gettin' mean. I want to know what you're doin' about it."

"Why should I do anythin'?" Con countered, his voice almost angry.

Ives's reply was so swift that it almost blended in with Con's last word. "Beth Hilliard is why!"

Con's gaze fell. He sat motionless, and Ives saw him smother a sigh. Ives put his glass on the desk and leaned back, watching, waiting.

"All right, I've seen it," Con said wearily. "What can I do?"

"What've you seen?"

It was Con's turn to cast back in his mind, remembering the small things.

"One thing sticks out," Con said slowly, his voice puzzled even now. "When I heard that Chevron had had a hell of a winter I went over to see Jess. I offered to let him have some money. He turned me down, kind of proud about it too." He shook his head. "I ain't tellin' this right, Ives. It sounds like a man bein' too proud to take help, only he didn't do it like that. It was a mind-your-own-damn-business kind of pride, like I was a nuisance."

56

Ives nodded thoughtfully. Con reached over with his fat, thick fingers and drew a piece of paper from among several in a cubbyhole in his desk. "Then there's this," Con said. "Curley brung it up on the stage this morning."

Ives read the note, which said: CON – *Find this girl a job at the hotel and see that she stays in town.* JESS.

"What girl?" Ives asked.

"Mrs. Macy. Used to be Martha Benton. Tip Macy's wife. He died in a blizzard this winter. I got her a job, and now all I got to do is keep her in town." Con seemed outraged now and angry. "Me, keep her in town! What am I – Jess Gove's man or my own? I never kept any man or woman from doin' what they damned well pleased and I never will!"

Old Ives nodded, and Con was silent. His breathing was heavy, as if he were both excited and angry, which he was. Suddenly he turned his head, looking at the door.

Ives looked with him, saw nothing, and glanced back at Con. And then he understood. The barroom was dead quiet, and that, to any saloon owner, meant trouble.

Con came to his feet with an agility surprising for a man of his bulk and yanked open the door and waddled out, Ives behind him.

The first thing they saw was a stranger, a big man in worn and dusty clothes, standing at the upper end of the room. He rested his weight on the elbow that was on the bar, forearms out straight, big fist loosely clenched. The other hand was on his hip, and he was watching Pete Framm, Ed Seegrist, and the other Chevron hand. The men from Pitchfork and Star 33, having seen that this concerned only the three Chevron men who were sticking, had backed away from the bar.

Pete Framm had moved out almost into the middle of the room, caution in his face. Ed Seegrist stayed at the bar, the other Chevron hand behind him.

Con saw immediately what was shaping up, noting especially the careful set of Ed Seegrist's face, and he said swiftly, "Hold it!"

"You keep out of this," the stranger said. He didn't look at Con; he didn't seem angry, only positive.

Ed Seegrist said meagerly, "Put a gun on him, Con. Jess wants him."

Con was a man who invariably did his level best to break up a fight, but when he understood Ed Seegrist's words he settled back on his heels and put his shoulder against the door. "Let Jess take him then," he said stubbornly.

Ed Seegrist's surprised glance shifted to Con for a bare second, and the stranger smiled faintly. Slowly he came erect, and Ed Seegrist moved away from the bar, his attention narrowing on the stranger, studying him.

The stranger said, "Pete Framm, you stay out. It's Seegrist I want."

He took a slow step forward, watchful, and stopped.

Ed said angrily, "Come on, Pete! Get over by the stove, Ray!"

The third Chevron puncher moved slowly away from Seegrist, looked at Pete Framm, and then hauled up beside him. Ed Seegrist was wholly isolated now, and for the first time he sensed it.

"Pete!" he said harshly, a note of desperation in his voice.

Pete Framm was held motionless by indecision and his doubt kept Ray immobile beside him.

The stranger said gently, "Seegrist, if I don't have to shoot you first I aim to run you out of the country." And he added with a dry, biting humor, "After I finish this — if you can run."

Old Ives watched the stranger move forward, slow step by slow step, and he kept waiting for Seegrist to pull a gun. But Ed Seegrist was not a lone fighter, and Ives knew the stranger had guessed it, and he fleetingly admired the way the other two Chevron hands had been neutralized. And then Ed Seegrist backed up a step, and Ives knew he had lost.

Ed kept backing down the bar; the stranger

kept coming on, and Ed's face was wild with anger. "Pete!" he kept saying. "Pete, what you waitin' for?"

And then he was brought up against one of the chairs around the poker table, and that decided him. He grabbed the heavy chair, whirled it around and far over his head, and then lunged for the stranger.

With a kind of pleased surprise old Ives watched it explode. Quick as thought the stranger lunged, too, and he had been swift enough to get inside the arc of the downswinging chair. Ed's arm came down across the stranger's shoulders, and the chair was wrenched from his hands.

Grasping Ed around the body, the stranger half turned him, shoved him from him, and then swung twice, hard, at Ed's face. The first blow landed, turning Ed's head half around, and knocked him sprawling into Ray's knees. Both of them went down, and now Ray scrambled away, coming to his feet, making no effort to join the fight. Ed came to his knees now, and the stranger held off until he was standing and then he came in, and Ed met him the only way he could, slugging savagely. The crowd moved up, excited, silent.

For a time the two men stood toe to toe, neither giving way, and then Ed was jarred back. The stranger moved up, stubborn, implacable, reminding old Ives of a tough young gray wolf. He kept pumping, smashing, sledging blows into Ed's face, and each time they landed Ed would give ground, turning his head with the blow, trying to ride it, failing. And then all Ed's fight gave way; he covered his face with his elbows. But the stranger didn't quit, only shifted to Ed's midriff now. The second blow jackknifed Ed, and he fell back against the stove. It rocked with Ed's impact, and then, because his slack weight was still against it, went over. The long length of pipe rumbled, slid, and then crashed to the floor and buckled, a great cloud of soot mushrooming up from the floor and raining down from the ceiling.

Ed Seegrist lay on his back in the falling soot, too weary to move from under the length of pipe that lay across his middle.

Old Ives saw something then, something that came close to shocking him. The stranger came over, yanked Ed to his feet, turned him, grabbed him by the collar of his shirt and the seat of his pants, and pitched him through the swing doors. They slammed back on their hinges when Ed hit, and they heard his moaning grunt as he hit the plank walk outside.

The stranger put a supporting hand against the doorjamb and, his chest heaving with his deep breathing, turned and laid his wild gaze on the rest of them and on Pete Framm finally.

61

In his gray-green eyes was one of the plainest invitations to fight that old Ives had ever witnessed, and he saw Pete Framm read it right too.

"That ought to square it," Pete said.

The stranger lounged erect, shaking his head deliberately. "Not yet, Pete. You tell Arnie Chance I'll make Chevron sorry it ever saw me. Tell him I collected my horse tonight too."

"Be careful," Pete said.

"Tell him."

Old Ives's pulse quickened then as he saw the stranger glance over at Con, nod in a way that could be both thanks and apology, and step out into the night.

Nobody moved for some seconds, and then a Star 33 hand said softly, "I could get awful sick of him. Who the hell is he?"

Young Pete Framm looked blankly at the over-turned stove, then at the door, and then his glance shifted speculatively to Con. There was a cross-grained amusement in his reckless eyes then, and he walked swiftly toward the door. Old Ives was right behind him, and when the doors opened the front lamp from the saloon laid its square pattern on the boardwalk. Seegrist lay there where the stranger had thrown him.

Pete hauled up and looked at the tie rail, and then he swore angrily. But when he turned to

Ives he was laughing.

"That damn Indian took my horse."

But old Ives was gone into the night on a very personal errand.

Pete knelt by Ed Seegrist and turned him over and looked at his face. Soot was mixed with blood until Seegrist looked like some swollen-faced, blackened corpse.

Pete thought quietly, *That is what I call a beating up.* He thought fleetingly of Dave Wallace, whose name he had learned from the hotel register in Vermillion, and he decided he liked him. What Wallace had done tonight took a brand of nerve that Pete wasn't sure he had himself. The cause of Wallace's quarrel with Ed was obscure, but there was nothing obscure about the way he was settling it.

Pete turned and called, "Ray," and then, hearing horses on the street, turned his head.

The light coming out through the saloon windows vaguely lighted the street, and Pete saw a team and top buggy pull up. Jess Gove was leaning out of the buggy, and he called sharply, "Who is it, Pete?"

"Ed Seegrist."

Gove spoke to somebody in the buggy and then stepped out and came up to Pete, who rose. At that moment Ray stepped out from the saloon.

Gove came over and paused in front of Seegrist, looking down at him. *That's twice Gove's done this,* Pete thought; *he don't like it, either.*

"What was the trouble?" Gove asked.

"The same," Pete said dryly.

Gove looked up quickly, and Pete surprised a look of consternation on his face. "Wallace?"

"He came in and chose Ed and rode off on a Chevron horse."

Jess Gove was facing the light, his features plain to see, and Pete caught a swift anger that came and died in it.

"While you two did what?" Jess wanted to know.

"Watched. I got no quarrel with Wallace."

"Chevron's got a quarrel with him," Jess said gently. "You even let him get away on Ed's horse."

"My horse," Pete corrected.

"That's worse. Why did you?"

Pete couldn't have answered that if he'd wanted to, because in the answer would lie the history of his association with Chevron, which he didn't understand himself. His loyalty to it was superficial and only two months old. It had taken several scraps to win the respect of the crew, and when he'd won that respect he found he didn't want it. It was a hard-case crew, and Arnie Chance rode them with his hard-case ways. A man did his work and kept his mouth shut and took his pay and blew it, and none of

64

it was much fun. And because it wasn't, Pete had rejected helping Ed tonight; it was Ed's fight, not Chevron's, and oddly, during the scrap, his loyalty had been with Dave Wallace.

So in answer to Jess Gove's question Pete only shrugged and was silent.

"Buckley in there?" Gove asked. At Pete's nod Jess said, "That's Miss Hilliard in the buggy. Take her down to the hotel." He stepped past Pete into the saloon.

Pete went out to the buggy, said, "Evenin', Miss Hilliard," and climbed up into the seat and picked up the reins.

"What's happened?" Beth asked.

"Just a little ruckus," Pete answered evasively.

"But wasn't that Ed Seegrist?"

"Yes'm."

The horses started moving, and then Beth asked, "Was it that same man?"

"Yes'm."

It was only a short way to the hotel. Pete pulled up there and climbed out and handed Beth up the steep steps. By the time he had lifted out her valise she had gone up the steps and into the hotel.

When Pete came in a moment later Beth was standing in the middle of the small, dimly lighted lobby and was looking toward the side wall. Pete glanced over and saw Tom Hyam, who owned the hotel, asleep. Hyam had pulled up two lobby chairs facing each other and half lay in one, with his feet sprawled out on the other. His coat and collar were off, his slim hands folded across the pleated bosom of a soiled shirt. Awake, Tom Hyam was a surly, hard-drinking man whom Hilliard didn't like. Asleep now, the ghost of his youth was with him, and Pete saw the handsome cynical gambler in a face that was tired and worn.

Pete said, "I'll wake him."

"Can't we just take a key?" Beth asked.

Pete nodded and went over to the small desk by the stairs and lifted a key from the board. He led the way upstairs, and into the room, where he put down the valise and lighted the lamp.

When he turned he surprised Beth's glance appraising him. Caught, Beth smiled. "You're new with us, too, aren't you?" She put out her hand. "I'm Beth Hilliard."

Pete yanked off his hat and grinned and shook hands, telling her his name.

Beth said, "I wonder if you'd do one more thing for me, Pete. Jess said Martha Macy was working here. Do you suppose you could find her and tell her I'm here?"

Pete said he could and stepped out into the hall, closing the door behind him. In the two months since he'd worked for Chevron he'd found nothing about it he liked half so well as this friendly girl. It made him think of Chevron with a new tolerance. It was only on the stairs that the other thing came to him, and he stopped dead. Martha Macy! Why, that was the same name Dave Wallace had asked about in the restaurant in Vermillion. He thought of it a moment and could make nothing of it and went down into the lobby. Hyam was still asleep, and Pete tramped past him into the dark dining room, carefully picking his way past the long tables toward the kitchen, whose door showed light under it.

Pushing open the door, Pete stepped into the hot kitchen. The cook, a Mexican, was setting the night's bread. On the zinc drainboard by the sink a woman stood sorting silver, her back to him.

"I'm lookin' for Mrs. Macy," Pete announced.

The girl whirled, dropping the silver that was in her hand as she turned. There was alarm in her face now as she regarded Pete, and then it slowly drained away. She stooped and picked up the silver she had dropped. Pete, puzzled, regarded her carefully, and with his smile came a slow feeling of pleasure. Martha Macy was pretty, and she was young and she was tired, and Pete smiled out of pure friendliness. She was a small girl, with black straight hair that she had done in an artless knot atop her head to get it out of the way. The work flush in her cheeks couldn't disguise her weariness, and she didn't answer Pete's grin. Her eyes were big, dark, veiled with caution.

"Miss Hilliard says to tell you she's here. Number eight."

Martha Macy stared at him a moment and then said tonelessly, "All right."

She rolled down her sleeves, removed her apron, and walked past Pete without looking at him. He followed her out into the lobby, heading for the street door, but watching her as she climbed the stairs. Tom Hyam snorted faintly as Pete reached the porch.

Beth answered the knock on her door, and when she saw Martha she gave a cry of delight, put her arms around her, and hugged her. Martha's smile was automatic, and when Beth led her to the bed and sat her down and then stood away from her, looking at her, Martha sat there, tense, uneasy.

"It's been two years, Marty. You haven't changed much," Beth said.

"I have," Martha contradicted dully. "You haven't, Beth. You're prettier than ever."

"I'm so sorry about Tip, Marty," Beth murmured.

"Yes."

"What have you been doing?" Beth asked. There was something in Martha's voice so lifeless and beaten that Beth hurried away from the subject of Tip.

"Working," Martha said dully. "Just working."

"Has – has it been hard?"

The moment Beth spoke she regretted it. The look of unspeakable bitterness in Martha's eyes was a reproof that brought the color to Beth's cheeks.

"No," Martha said without irony. "Everybody's been good to me."

Beth sat down in the chair and asked simply, "What kind of work, Marty?"

"Waiting table. It hasn't been hard. I'm doing all right." While she spoke she didn't look at Beth. The dead indifference in her voice, in her face, almost terrified Beth. This wasn't the girl she had grown up with, the girl who could dance a night away with half the men on the western slope, whose favor had caused a hundred fist fights, who had married a steady, reliable man to prove her good sense. Misfortune alone couldn't do this to her; it was something else, and Beth wanted to know what it was.

"Marty, what's wrong?" Beth asked suddenly.

She saw the shock of the question in Martha's face. "Why, nothing, Beth. What could be?"

Beth made up her mind swiftly. "Marty, you're coming home with me to the ranch. Lord knows how long it'll be for, but you're welcome to stay until we sell. You need a rest."

"I couldn't, Beth. Thanks." Martha didn't look at her.

"But you've got to!"

"No!" Martha said flatly, almost harshly. "I couldn't do it."

Beth rose and came over and sat down beside her. "Try it for a week, Marty. After that maybe things will look better."

Martha shook her head, and when she looked at Beth there was alarm in her eyes. "Please, Beth, I'm all right! I like working. I — I'd be lost without it."

"But what's wrong?" Beth asked gently.

Martha came quickly to her feet. "Nothing, nothing! Why don't you let me alone!" Her dark eyes were blazing with anger. *She's cornered,* Beth thought. *What have I said?*

Beth was silent, and when Martha saw she wasn't going to answer she relaxed a little, and the bitterness crept back into her face.

"I'm sorry, Beth," she said flatly. "Just let me alone. Nothing's wrong. I'm — just different. Don't try to change me."

"All right," Beth said gently.

Martha walked over to the door, opened it, and then turned. She looked as if she were about to speak; there was a softness, almost a pleading in her eyes, and Beth waited breathlessly for her to speak.

Then it was gone. "Good night, Beth," she

said, and she closed the door behind her.

Downstairs Pete waited until she had gone into the kitchen again, and then he went back, too, passing Hyam, still asleep, on the way.

When he stepped into the kitchen Martha Macy was alone. The cook had gone for the night.

She eyed Pete over her shoulder with quiet hostility, and when he let the door close behind him she straightened and turned from her work.

"What do you want?"

Pete put his shoulder against the wall. "Nothin' much," he said quietly. "There's a man around here lookin' for you. I thought you might want to know."

Suspicion was plain in Martha's face, but her hands were still. "Who?"

"Fella name of Dave Wallace."

The name moved her. Pete could see her breathing slow down, see the bright lift in her eyes. She turned abruptly to her work. "I don't know him," she said.

"He's raisin' a lot of hell around here," Pete murmured. "He's liable to get hurt. I thought you'd better tell him."

Martha looked squarely at him. "I told you I didn't know him."

"Sure."

He didn't move, and Martha went on sorting

silver. But her pace slowed presently, and then her hands ceased working. She stared at her hands and asked softly, "Who's going to hurt him?"

"Chevron."

Martha looked obliquely at him. "Haven't I seen you with Chevron?"

"I work for it."

Martha looked full at him now, seeing a young, brash puncher with a troubled seriousness in his face. "Did Jess tell you he'd get hurt?"

"No. I can tell."

"I don't know him," Martha reiterated.

Pete shifted away from the wall, and he spoke slowly. "I get to town now and then. Reckon I could see you some time?"

"No," Martha said flatly.

She looked at Pete for a full ten seconds, and he could not read her glance. A quick grin flashed across his face as he put on his Stetson. "I aim to change your mind," he said. "Good night."

And he went out through the dark dining room. Stepping into the lobby, he glanced at Tom Hyam and was surprised to find the hotel owner's eyes open, watching him.

"Come here, you," Hyam said quietly.

Pete stopped, arrested by the tone of Hyam's voice. Hyam stared at him, his dark eyes bland

72

and contemptuous.

"Leave that girl alone," Hyam said flatly. He didn't move, lay slack in one chair with his feet in the other.

"And who says I will?" Pete drawled.

"I do."

"You got to say it louder than that," Pete murmured.

Hyam yawned and closed his eyes, and presently Pete, baffled and angry, stepped out into Hilliard's night. This country and its people, he decided abruptly, took some figuring, and he was a man for it.

CHAPTER 5

Dave came awake at bare dawn. He had been sleeping on his side, knees drawn to chest, and he didn't move against the morning chill that was seeping through his thin blankets. This was the spot he had picked last night in the dark after fleeing Hilliard, and now he regarded it with curiosity. It was a small break in the pine and aspen timber, and a thin ground mist still clung close to the earth. Beyond, some forty feet away in a like clearing, he had staked out his stolen Chevron horse, and now he lifted his head off his rolled-up slicker, looking sleepily for the horse.

He could see the whole clearing, and the horse was gone.

He boiled out of his blankets and came to his stocking feet, sleep shocked out of him. The horse wasn't there.

"I staked him out in a little meadow below," a voice said.

Dave wheeled in his tracks. There, hunkered down against the base of a big jack pine, was a man. He was the color of an Indian and, save for his close-cropped gray hair and pale eyes, looked like one. Dave regarded him carefully, searching his memory, and behind thought he was calculating the exact spot where his gun rested under his slicker.

"You were in the saloon last night," Dave said finally.

"That's right." Old Ives paused a moment and then said, "Pick up your gun if it'll make you feel better. I'm alone, though."

Dave considered him a moment and then asked, "You haven't got anything to eat with you, have you?"

"It's waitin' over yonder where I camped last night."

Dave said quickly, "Where you camped?"

"I found you last night," Ives said idly. "I figured you needed some sleep."

Dave had a moment of feeling foolish, and he covered it by sitting on his blankets and pulling on his boots. His hunger was so insistent that it didn't leave much room for anything else, but he was trying stubbornly to find a reason for this visit. His boots on, he strapped on his gun belt, and old Ives rose without a word and set off into the timber, Dave behind him.

Less than a hundred yards away and uphill was old Ives's camp. He had a fire going, and a full two-cup coffeepot and three quarters of a bannock were warming by the fire.

"I've et," Ives said. "Tie into it."

Dave did, and the coarse salty bread tasted like cake to him. He had had one full meal yesterday and one the day before, and the prospects of his next one were uncertain. While he ate he watched Ives prowl around the camp in that swift, silent way and finally disappear in the timber. Dave, with the edge of his hunger blunted, regarded the old man's outfit and tried to peg him and couldn't. He wasn't a puncher, and he traveled light and simple, like an Indian.

When Ives came back leading both their horses and tied them close, Dave was finished eating and was smoking his after-breakfast cigarette. The sun was touching the tops of the distant trees, and everywhere he looked the jack pines and popples and underbrush seemed washed and fresh as newly minted coins.

Dave said, half in apology, "I've cleaned you out."

"I can get more, and you can't," Ives grunted. He came over to the fire, shoved the unburned ends of the wood in, and hunkered down on his hams. His close scrutiny of Dave was embarrassing for a moment until he asked bluntly, "What do you do now?"

"I don't know," Dave said, making his voice neutral. "What should I?"

"Ride out of the country."

Dave shook his head and offered Ives his sack of tobacco. Ives rolled a smoke, his face musing, and handed Dave the tobacco and afterward lighted his cigarette with a coal from the fire, which he handled as if it were not even warm.

"Tell me about this," Ives said then.

"Wait a minute," Dave protested. "I don't know you — not even your name."

"Ives. I'm a wolfer. I been waitin' a long time for somebody to name Chevron. Last night, when you done it, I wanted to talk to you."

"Why?"

"To find out why you done it," Ives said cautiously.

Dave was silent for a moment, feeling his hunch. There was nothing indirect or subtle about Ives; he'd come to the point without subterfuge, and Dave had an unaccountable feeling that Ives wasn't just curious, that he was asking questions with a purpose in mind.

Dave said, "You trapped wolves in this country last winter?"

Ives nodded.

"Tell me," Dave said slowly. "Was it a winter that would kill a man?"

"Depends on the man."

"This man was raised in the Montana high country, and he thought like an Indian."

"No," Ives said promptly. "It was a bad winter, but only for cattlemen. They bog a horse down in the snow and then try and drag him to a line shack. They'll sweat a sheepskin into ice and freeze their feet in them dancin' boots. Any damn one of 'em I ever saw will fight a blizzard and get spooked when —" Ives's voice trailed off, and he looked sharply at Dave. "Oh," he said gently. "Him."

Dave nodded. "Did you know him?"

"Macy? No. I just heard about him yesterday. I never paid it no mind."

Dave didn't say anything, and Ives rubbed his jaw thoughtfully, staring out into the timber. "So you don't believe a blizzard killed him?"

"Would you?"

"You was a friend of his and knew him?"

"That's right."

"I don't reckon I would," Ives said. "Still, he's dead, and bein' so, why is he?"

"That's what I come to find out," Dave answered quietly, and he told him about meeting Seegrist across the desert, about losing his horse at the dry Bunchgrass Tanks, about finding Ed Seegrist in Vermillion and tangling with him. And then he told him about Sheriff Kinsley and Arnie Chance, of them moving Martha Macy to Hilliard, and his exit from Vermillion, and as he talked his voice got flat and almost hard. "So how does that add up?" he asked when he'd finished.

Ives asked obliquely, "What'd you come to Hilliard for?"

"To see Mrs. Macy."

"Did you?"

Dave shook his head.

"Why not?" Ives asked.

"I saw Seegrist first," Dave said.

Ives spat and looked boldly at Dave. "Couldn't pass up the chance to kick the hell out of him, is that it?"

"I told him I would."

"Sure you did," Ives prodded. "You come into this country because you doubted if Macy died in a blizzard. You wanted to talk to his wife. You know his wife knows somethin', because Gove's tryin' to hide her. And then, by God when you get the chance to talk to her, with nobody to stop you, you have a jangle with one of Gove's punchers. You steal his horse and you ride off without seein' Macy's wife." Ives spat. "Hell, you're just a dumb, tough puncher, like all of 'em. Gove'll tree you and nail up your hide before you ever get a look at Mrs. Macy."

There was enough truth in what he said to make Dave wince. He said grimly, "Take it easy, old-timer, I'll see her."

"Like hell you will," Ives jeered. "You'll be five hundred miles from here with Gove on your tail before you ever stop to think you didn't see her."

Ives rose and kicked dirt on the fire and then turned to his horse.

Dave said, "You didn't come here to tell me that."

Ives paused and eyed him sourly. "I thought I could help you. But not after this."

Dave came to his feet and went over to Ives. "I need help," he said slowly.

"Hah!" Ives jeered. "Not you — not Jack the Giant Killer."

A swift anger mounted in Dave and then subsided. He'd thought this crotchety old wolfer might help him, but now he knew it was useless to expect it. Ives had a grudge against Chevron and Gove, and Dave could use a man with a grudge. But not this one. It would be like tying up with a buzz saw. Dave left him and turned to his horse and stepped into the saddle without a word.

"I'll leave some grub here tonight," Ives said sourly. "It'll be enough to take you out of the country."

"Keep it," Dave said, and he rode out of camp.

When he was gone old Ives's seamed face cracked into a broad grin. He danced a little jig behind his mare, and when she turned her head to look at him Ives laughed softly.

"By all that's holy," he whispered. "By all that's holy, I bet I've found him."

For old Ives had a philosophy that was applied in reverse. He believed profoundly that hate got more things done than did love, that taunts and ridicule were surer weapons than praise, that a prod was better than a pull. And he wanted Dave Wallace, but he had to be sure of him.

Dave put his horse into the timber, and by the time he had fully smoked down a cigarette he was able to smile grimly at what had taken place. The truth of Ives's words still rankled. It was true he'd missed Martha Macy, whom he wanted to talk to. It was equally true that Seegrist had sent him out in the desert to die and that he had promised to settle with Seegrist for it. Gove had heard him, and Chance had heard him, and because they had he was going through with it, Ives or no Ives, because it was his way. But if Ives thought that his fight with Chevron was more important than the discovery of how Tip had really died, he was wrong.

He came to the meadow where Ives had staked out his horse last night, and with instinctive caution he skirted it. He wished he knew how much of an uproar his fight with Seegrist had caused. Would he be hunted, or would Gove want to settle with him?

Presently the timber thinned out and Dave

81

reined up on the lip of a gentle grade. Below him, where the timber broke away into a grassy park, he saw the wagon road that would take him to Hilliard, or to Vermillion and the desert below. He hit the road and put his horse up the grade toward Hilliard, neither realizing nor caring that he had made his choice and that it would be too late to turn back after this.

By daylight Hilliard had the drabness of a high mountain town that wasn't worth the paint to brighten it. Dave put his horse down the steep road into the canyon bottom, and there was a chill gloom here that wouldn't lift until the midday sun touched it.

The chatter of the Little Dun dimly filled the air. A hammering downstreet was answered by a quick echo from the close walls, and the smoke from the breakfast fires drifted lazily toward the north, moved by a cold current of air from the stream.

At the small stable and corral which Dave had to pass first a couple of men eyed him blankly as he rode by. The Chevron brand on the left hip of his chestnut was plain to see, and he was content to let them make what they would of it. There was little risk of meeting Chevron here at this hour, yet he was watchful as he rode past the scattering of log shacks toward the larger buildings that crowded the narrow street. This was not a woman's town, Dave observed; most of the things in it were there to serve men. The large store was built without shop windows, after the fashion of the trading posts in the Indian country. Between it and the hotel at the head of the street were a barbershop and a blacksmith's weathered shed with a rotting wooden watering trough by its door.

A freight wagon was pulled up beside an ancient warehouse across the street, and its five teams almost reached to the timber bridge. A pair of teamsters were loading the empty beer barrels stacked in front of the Olympus, rolling them on the plank walk the dozen feet to the wagon. Beyond the Olympus was a squat building that contained a lone billiard table, and this room opened on to a restaurant, whose front bore the legend: Eats and Billiards. Save for a lone buckboard pulled sidewise to the hitch rail in front of the store across the street, the tie rails were empty.

Dave dismounted in front of the Olympus, skirted the barrels and shouldered through the saloon's swing doors.

A lone drinker eyed him in the flaked back-bar mirror as he approached the bar, his boots ringing solidly on the floor.

Con Buckley, in shirt sleeves and wearing a vast apron, left the office and started for the bar. When he caught sight of Dave he stopped abruptly, and for some seconds his face was bland with a controlled surprise.

"Nice morning," Dave said.

Con came slowly to the end of the bar and folded his fat arms on the bar top. He said, "They're huntin' you."

"I want to ask a question."

"It better be short," Con said in a neutral voice. "They're apt to drift in here any time."

Dave nodded. "Where's Martha Macy?"

So that's what's behind Jess Gove's order, Con thought swiftly. He tilted his head in the direction of the other man. "Workin' for him."

Dave turned his head to regard the other man, who was listening to the conversation. Dave took in the soiled shirt, the handsome face slack with dissolute living, the insolent eyes that had not even the saving grace of being shrewd. A beaten gambler, he thought, and waited for him to speak.

"Not since this morning," Hyam said. "She left this morning with Jess Gove and Miss Hilliard for Chevron."

Dave knew a swift despair then, thinking: *Ives was right. I'm too late.* He pushed away from the bar, murmuring his thanks, and caught Buckley's deep shrewd gaze on him.

"Thanks for last night," he said.

"I won't do it again," Buckley said.

"You won't have to."

Dave stepped out onto the plank walk, and

84

already he was pushing toward a hard decision. He was thinking that if Martha Macy was with Beth Hilliard and they were both with Gove, then Gove couldn't move against him in the presence of the two women. He wasn't dead sure of this, so he remembered Beth Hilliard as best he could, recalling her few words to him, the set of her eyes, the honest look of her. He was careful about this, because it was important, and when he came to his decision he went out to his horse.

The two men who had watched him from the stable were now leaning against the front of the Olympus, eyeing him. Dave stepped into the saddle and said to them, "Where's Chevron?"

One man was too surprised to answer. The other said, "You're ridin' one of their horses."

"I'm returning it."

The man told him, and Dave rode out across the timber bridge and up the grade to the higher country.

When Dave was out of sight Con Buckley turned away from the window. He laid his speculative gaze on Tom Hyam and was sorry this had happened in front of him. Hyam was new here; and Con Buckley distrusted him. Hyam would talk, and the word would get to Gove. Last night had been bad enough. He'd refused to help Seegrist, and Gove had asked him why. That conversation hadn't been pleasant, although there were no threats made. It had seemed to Buckley, though, that Gove was close to anger. And Chevron, broke or rich, was something Con didn't like to buck, both for sentimental and practical reasons.

He went into his office and came out with a bottle of his favorite Irish whisky. He set it on the bar, put out two glasses and poured them full, and looked at Hyam. "Like to try it?"

Hyam nodded. They drank off the whisky, and Hyam smacked his lips appreciatively.

Con put the bottle away and crossed his thick arms on the bar.

"You might call that a bribe," he said.

Hyam raised his eyebrows.

"Just forget what the big fellow said, will you? I'm supposed to be neutral here. I try to be."

"Afraid of Gove?" Hyam asked, smiling a little.

"Just careful."

Hyam shrugged and said, "Suits me."

CHAPTER 6

Seen from the desert floor the great bulk of the Dun River Range had seemed to climb sheer, its timbered shoulders vaulting abruptly to the snow fields which stubbornly clung into this late spring. But traveling the stage road that eventually crossed the range in a low pass beneath the peaks, Dave adjusted his opinion. The western slope of the Duns was a long gradient which began at Vermillion, crossed the rich grass flats into fold after mounting fold of foothills, and, above Hilliard, lifted into sheer climbs that broke onto broad grass-floored valleys. It was a rough country here, high and wild and unfenced, and after the sun disappeared in mid-morning there was that chill conifer-and-black-earth smell about it which the rains seemed to draw out of the rugged pelt of these mountains.

Dave passed the first road that turned off into the Pitchfork and caught a glimpse of small valleys where cattle were grazing. They were fat, their winter coats ragged and shedding now, and they eyed him with a kind of wary contentment as he rode by. Now he forded and reforded the Little Dun in a heavily timbered slope. The savage winter had left its mark here, for the aspens were bent to the ground, some of them broken. The Little Dun had vaulted its bed in the spring, and there were the marks of its high water on the tree trunks.

Presently the grade leveled off and the timber broke, and Dave reined up at its edge. A long open valley, its hummocks a deep cold green with the new grass, stretched off to the shoulder of a bare granite escarpment far to the south, and below this Dave saw the clutter of low log buildings that was the Chevron.

As he rode closer the buildings sorted themselves out, leaving the house isolated with three towering pines behind it. It was built of hewn logs, except for one section that was the core of it and which Dave guessed had been the original house of peeled timbers. It was one story, multiroomed and sprawling, and thrust up through the thick grass as naturally as the trees from which it was built. To the west of it, on the gentle downgrade to the cup of the valley, lay first the combination bunkhouse and cookshack, and beyond it the wagon-shed barn and corrals. The fenced horse pasture edged from the corrals to the little feeder creek in its valley bottom that reached the Dun at the far end of the valley.

When Dave crossed the plank bridge in front of the house his horse's shoes clattered warning, and before he was much farther a man stepped out from the barn, another from the bunkhouse. Dave watched the house now and saw nothing, although blue smoke from a fire was rising slowly into the chill air.

He heard the man by the bunkhouse say something over his shoulder, and then the puncher at the barn started to run toward the wagon shed, to a corner of which a horse was tied.

They recognized him, Dave knew, and he waited for the first one to drift up to the house to announce his presence. They did not, however.

Riding into the place, he headed for the bunkhouse and reined up there. The puncher who stood by the barn was Ray, the one who'd been with Pete last night.

Dave folded his arms and leaned on the saddle horn and said, "I've got a horse of yours."

Ray was so bewildered he opened his mouth to answer and no words came out. Now Dave turned his head, hearing men running, and then Arnie Chance and Pete Framm rounded the corner of the cookshack and immediately slowed into a walk. The puncher who had run for the horse was mounted now, and he circled wide, putting himself between Dave and the bridge. It was quick, neat, thorough, Dave thought.

"He brung the horse back," Ray announced blankly.

Arnie Chance didn't even look at Ray. He came up to Dave's horse, put a hand on the bridle, and then looked up at him. Another puncher slipped out of the bunkhouse and circled behind Dave.

Arnie Chance's eyes were bloodshot, the lids puffed, and his lean cheeks had a heavy, blond-rust beard stubble on them. Dave remembered the saloonkeeper's words, "They're lookin' for you," and he supposed Arnie Chance had got little sleep last night.

Dave said, "I'm still looking for Martha Macy."

"Are you, now?" Arnie Chance drawled mockingly. "Well, step in and wait for her."

"Gove here?"

"He'll wish he had been," Chance said, and he laughed.

For the first time Dave had a feeling something was wrong.

Arnie said, "Pete, get Ed out here."

Dave's gaze shifted to Pete Framm, and what he read there was disquieting. The dismay in Pete's lean face as he started toward the bunkhouse was plain, and Dave's pulse quickened. He stared down placidly at Chance and said, "While I'm about it, I'd like to talk to Miss Hilliard, too."

"Take your time," Chance drawled, not even looking at Dave.

Ed Seegrist appeared in the doorway now. The shock of fear on his battered face when he saw Dave was observed by every one of them. He licked his swollen lips and started to back into the bunkhouse and was blocked by Pete Framm.

"Take a look at him," Chance said contemptuously. "Here's the hard case you aimed to run away from."

Ed said softly, weakly, "Yeah."

"He don't look nine feet tall to me," Chance said dryly. He paused. "What are you goin' to do?"

"Nothin'," Seegrist whispered.

Dave realized now that last night's beating, coupled with the threat that Pete had repeated to Seegrist, had had its effect. Seegrist was genuinely afraid of him.

"Think again," Chance drawled.

Seegrist looked beseechingly at each of the crew, and his face was ashen. He held out his hand to Pete and whispered, "Give me your gun."

"Oh no," Chance said quickly, flatly.

"Nothin' like that." He looked up at Dave, a deep malice in his bleach eyes. "Step down," he invited.

Dave looked past Ed Seegrist's battered face to Pete and saw Pete was watching him. Pete shook his head imperceptibly, and Dave knew immediately bleakly, that he had made a mistake. Gove wasn't here, and neither was Beth Hilliard.

Chance said sharply, "Pete. Go get a singletree for Ed. We'll see if he can beat some of the salt out of this hard case."

Dave acted with blind haste then. He roweled his horse savagely, and as the horse jumped Dave freed his foot from his right stirrup and kicked savagely at Arnie Chance's head. His kick landed with a shock that numbed his foot, and he kneed his horse into the foreman. Chance went down, knocked rolling by the frightened horse. Dave hugged the neck of his horse and put him toward the end of the shack. Somebody was alert. A gun went off behind him, and a long sliver was chipped out of a heavy log by the corner.

Dave rounded the corner of the building now and for a moment was safe from the men afoot. The puncher on the horse, however, lit out after him, shooting now as Dave, flat on his pony's neck, headed for the wagon shed some seventy yards away.

He did not expect to make it, and he knew he would not, when he heard two other guns join in with the mounted puncher's. But he watched the shed approach and was kicking his legs free of the stirrups to jump when his horse simply folded under him. Dave went over his head; he heard the horse do a complete somersault, jarring the ground as he landed, and then Dave hit. He tried to land rolling, but the full force of the impact was on his shoulder, and then his face was mashed in the dirt by the weight of him, and all the breath was driven from his lungs.

Dimly he heard the rider pounding down on him, and in a kind of panic he pushed himself over on his back and rolled toward the shed.

His fall had thrown him within a few feet of the wagon shed, and the rider, unable to stop his horse, swerved away from Dave to miss the shed and at the same time shot.

Dave came to his knees and, stumbling and falling and rising again, he made the open end of the shed and fell inside. He still had no breath, and he fought to drag air into his tortured lungs, lying there in the dust and yanking weakly at his gun. He heard the rider circle the shed, coming back for him, and when he pounded past the door Dave shot. It was a miss and the rider went on, scared off, and now Dave, getting his first breath, pulled himself to the corner and poked his gun around it and shot at the three men running toward him.

He shot three times, unable to see for the swimming darkness that clouded his sight. But Arnie Chance was no fool; he had swiftly calculated the distance left to the shed and it was too far, and he angled off, diving behind the pile of saw logs away from the cookshack. One of his punchers stopped and turned tail, while the other circled widely to the other side of the bunkhouse. The rider had kept on and was now in the shelter of the barn a hundred feet away.

Dave came shakily to his knees, hurriedly shucking the empties out of his gun and slipping in new cartridges from his belt. He backed up now, so that he was out of the line of fire from the barn almost in front of him and peered through the chink in the logs at the bunkhouse and cookshack.

He heard Arnie Chance bawl, "Keep Ed away from a horse." And then he shouted for rifles, ordering his men to places which would effectively surround the shed. Dave's downed horse lay there, trying to fight to its knees and unable to.

Breathing deeply, shakily, Dave wiped the dirt from the corner of his mouth and knelt against the inside wall, taking stock, listening. It gave him a vicious pleasure to know that he had terrified Seegrist into running. Last night's beating had been more thorough than he supposed. A chill wind stirred coldly past the shed, and he shivered.

Someone by the bunkhouse opened up with a Sharps now; Dave could spot its booming grunt, feel the jar of its heavy slug when it hit the log. He came to his feet, moved to the back of the shed, and pulled moss from a chink so he could see out. This, he thought narrowly, was a fool's fight. He could have got off with an unholy beating and cracked head if he hadn't bolted. Now they were out to get him, and it was merely a matter of time.

It had begun with a question asked idly at the far edge of the desert, and it had trapped him in a wagon shed on a high-country ranch, and still he did not know the answer to the question of how Tip Macy had died. The irony of it brought a cold anger to his eyes and with it the certain knowledge that Jess Gove and his crew would kill the man who insisted on the answer.

He heard the fire slack off, and then Arnie Chance's angry voice called: "You ain't got a chance, Wallace. Better come out."

Dave didn't answer, and Arnie waited a moment, then shouted, "One more time, Wallace. You comin' out?"

Deep inside him a hard bedrock of common

sense told Dave to quit, that it wasn't worth it. But there was old Ives and a thickheaded sheriff and the memory of the shock and despair at the Bunchgrass Tanks and of words he had spoken, and beyond all this was an obstinate pride that went deeper than sense.

He called, "I don't reckon."

They opened up from three sides then, and Dave, shooting through the chinks in the logs, kept Arnie Chance down behind the saw logs and patiently watched the barn and the open side of the shed.

Presently, from the back, and close, a new rifle opened up. Dave saw the moss fly from the chink close to his knee, and he knew this rifleman was going about it systematically.

He bellied down against the base log now, and he was quiet with a patient dismal fatalism. This had held to a pattern whose end he had read, but now that he had reached it, he found it hard to accept, as a man always refuses to look at death until it is with him. It was just after midday now; with luck, he could hold them off until dark. After that Arnie Chance could finish it whenever he chose. He listened to them hammering away at the shed, knowing they were still too angry for guile.

And then abruptly the firing ceased. Somewhere off in the mountains thunder rolled distantly. Dave raised his head and peered out through the chink between the logs.

Pulled up by the bunkhouse was a top buggy. Jess Gove stepped down and headed swiftly for the pile of saw logs, Beth Hilliard behind him.

She followed Jess over to where Arnie Chance was forded up and she almost ran.

There was a hard argument now, and Arnie Chance came to his feet, brushing the chips off his denim pants, not looking at Gove.

It was Beth Hilliard who turned now and walked swiftly toward the wagon shed. As she passed Dave's horse, dead now, she slowed, then hurried on.

When she rounded the corner of the shed she hauled up and saw Dave flattened against the back wall, his gun held loosely in his hand. She wore a man's suit coat over her dress against the high-country chill.

"Are you all right?" she asked swiftly.

"So far," Dave said dryly. "You want me to step out, where your boys can hit me?"

"Come with me," Beth said.

Dave walked out to her and saw immediately that she was white with anger. He still held the gun in his hand and swung in beside her, and they went back to Gove and Chance. Gove's benign, kindly face still held a shock; he stood there, shoulders stooped, both hands on his hips, gravely watching Beth approach. Chance eyed her sullenly and then shifted his gaze to

Dave. His eyes were hot, wicked. His cheek was cut and bleeding where Dave's boot had caught him. Seegrist had disappeared.

Beth Hilliard said angrily, "I want to know what happened here, Arnie."

"That cocky son rode in here on a stole horse, and when we asked him about it he kicked me in the head."

Dave said flatly, "Chance invited me to get down and take a beating with a singletree. I didn't cotton to it."

"What are you here for?" Beth asked angrily of Dave.

Dave lifted his gaze to Jess Gove, who was watching him carefully, intently. "Gove knows. So does Chance. You might ask them."

Beth looked from Jess to Arnie, as if waiting for them to speak, and when they didn't she turned again to Dave. Her voice was stubborn, still angry. "You knocked down Ed Seegrist the first time you saw him. You beat him up last night in town. Will you tell me, in plain words, what this is all about?"

"Sure, I'll tell you," Dave drawled. "I met Ed Seegrist across the desert and saw him riding a Chevron-branded horse. I asked him how Tip Macy died. He lied and he sent me out to a water hole he knew was dry. You picked me up four days afterward — afoot, but still alive."

"How Tip Macy died?" Beth asked blankly.

"Do you know how he died?" Dave countered.

Beth Hilliard was honestly puzzled. Her hazel eyes were wide as she studied Dave during a second's silence. Then she said, "He got caught in a blizzard."

"That's the story," Dave said dryly.

"It's not true?"

"No."

Beth eyed him sharply, her face alert. Then she looked over at Gove, who didn't take his glance from Dave.

"Why do you say that?" Beth asked.

"I lived with him for two winters in the Montana high country," Dave murmured. "He knew blizzards."

"That's strange proof!" Beth said angrily.

"It's enough to start on," Dave replied calmly. "I've got more. But maybe Gove and Chance don't want to hear it."

"I want to hear it!" Beth said angrily. "Macy worked for me as much as Jess or Arnie! And I'm a friend of his wife, Martha Macy."

"Then maybe you'd let me talk to her," Dave murmured dryly. "Gove and Chance won't."

That seemed to check Beth's anger. She was speechless a moment, not understanding, and then she said, "I don't know what that means."

Dave smiled crookedly, watching Gove. "The night I got into Vermillion I looked for Martha

Macy. She'd been put on the stage for Hilliard — the same stage we came in on. I was eased out of town by Chance and Sheriff Kinsley next morning. I came to Hilliard. As soon as Gove found out I was still in the country he moved her out of Hilliard."

"That's not so!" Beth said swiftly. "She's visiting Harriet Bell at Pitchfork today."

"Sure," Dave said dryly. "She's always somewhere else when I want to see her. Gove or Chance sees to that. Ask them."

Beth turned to Jess now, putting the answer up to him.

And then, surprisingly, mildly, Gove said, "That's right."

"But — why?" Beth asked.

Gove said matter-of-factly, "You and Wallace go up to the office, Beth. I've got something there to show you both. I'll be along in a minute."

Beth hesitated, then looked at Dave, and started toward the house. He fell in beside her, passing the silent, hostile crew, and rounding the corner of the bunkhouse. There was a constraint between them that Dave made no effort to put aside. He was certain now that she had never known of Gove's attempt to keep Martha Macy from seeing him. He wondered what dodge Gove would present.

Beth, in her impatience, was a little ahead, so

100

Dave could look at her, and he liked the straight way she walked. The man's coat she was wearing made her shoulders seem wider, and the way her hands were fisted in her pockets made Dave think she was more used to denim pants and a man's coat than a dress.

Beth entered a room in the wing closest the bunkhouse. It was the ranch office, Dave could see, a big desk littered with papers, deep leather armchairs, and a cast-off sofa made up the homely furnishings.

The gathering afternoon storm had shut off the light, and Beth went straight to the lamp on the desk and lighted it.

Then she turned and motioned Dave to a chair. He sat down, holding his Stetson in his hand, and they regarded each other carefully.

Beth said suddenly, "It's been very queer meetings between us."

"Yes'm," Dave said.

"I keep remembering what you said about Jess Gove that night on the hotel gallery," Beth said. She sank into the chair by the desk, watching Dave gravely. "You remember?"

Dave nodded.

"I'd still like to know why you said it."

"I said it because I didn't know Gove was your partner," Dave drawled. "If I'd known it I don't reckon I would have."

"You were wrong, you know."

101

"Nothing I've seen makes me believe I was," Dave said stubbornly.

"You mean you think I'm a fool to trust him as a partner?"

"Is that a question, ma'am?"

"Yes."

"Yes."

"You're insulting," Beth said angrily.

"You asked," Dave said idly. He surveyed the room in a leisurely manner, not looking at her, aware that she was angry and hoping that she was seeing how foolish this conversation was. He didn't want anything from Chevron except an explanation of Tip Macy's death — if it could be explained.

Gove came in then, stooping for the door. He threw his hat on the sofa and went over to the desk. He looked tired as he fumbled among the papers there. Beth, to allow him room, rose and crossed to the sofa. She gave Dave an unfriendly glance as she passed him.

Gove found the paper, put a pair of iron-rimmed spectacles on and read it, then sat down, holding the paper in his lean hand.

He spoke to Beth now, "I didn't expect to have to tell you this, Beth. It won't make you happy. But Wallace is persistent about something that may or may not concern him."

He looked at Dave. "I'm telling you something that even Sheriff Kinsley doesn't know."

Dave said nothing.

Gove said, "Tip Macy didn't die in a blizzard. He was shot."

There was a moment of stillness in the room that Dave didn't break. He waited, watching Gove. It was Beth who spoke.

"But, Jess! Tip Macy? Shot?"

Gove nodded and went on calmly: "On the twelfth of January, when Tip was supposed to report in from the boundary-line camp and didn't, we waited a couple of days, then sent a man after him. He was found just outside the door of the shack, a bullet through his back. There was a foot of snow over him."

Beth didn't ask any questions now. She listened, transfixed.

"The man who found him, Seegrist, didn't touch him. He got Chance and myself, and we went to look at him. We searched him first. Among the usual stuff, we found this in his pocket."

He leaned over and handed the piece of paper to Dave. Beth rose and came over and stood beside Dave, reading over his shoulder. The paper was small, stained a dull brown.

Gove said wearily, "It's a bill of sale for thirty head of Chevron cattle, signed by me. Trouble is, my signature is a poor forgery."

"What does it mean?" Beth asked swiftly.

Gove shrugged tiredly. "Nobody can be sure,

but we can tell what it points to. All the evidence shows that Tip Macy was selling stolen Chevron beef to some of the riffraff over on the reservation and was forging my name to the bills of sale so they could ship them."

Dave rejected this instantly, without thought, with only instinct to serve him. Tip never stole a cow in his life. His face did not alter as he looked up and waited for Gove to proceed.

"Apparently," Gove said, "the buyers and Tip quarreled. They shot him, then rode off, not bothering to search him. We found this in his shirt pocket."

Dave thought quietly, *Play it careful, careful,* and he said nothing. Beth Hilliard would ask all the questions.

She had been holding a corner of the bill of sale. Now, understanding the brown stain on the paper, she slowly withdrew her hand. She stood by Dave then and said softly, "Poor Martha. Poor, poor Martha."

Gove nodded gloomily. "We weren't going to tell her, but we had to. She said, like Wallace here, that Tip couldn't have died in a blizzard. But outside of Martha, nobody knows how Tip died, not even Kinsley." He added softly, his voice tired and kind, "We all love Martha. There was no sense in shaming her if we could help it."

Beth said gently, "Jess, that was kind of you.

She's so proud. She was so proud of Tip, too. It would have hurt her terribly."

Gove nodded. "It would have, and nobody would have gained by it." Now he looked at Dave. "That's why we've tried to keep you from seeing her. You would have hounded her into telling you, and then her secret would no longer be a secret. You can see that?"

Dave nodded.

"I'll ask you to keep it then," Gove said. He paused and added mildly, "I'll also ask you not to see her. You know how Macy died, which is what you came for. Bothering Martha, reminding her of it, talking with her won't do any good. She wants to forget. Besides that, I've given her my word I wouldn't tell a living soul. I've broken that word by telling you and Beth, and I wouldn't like her to know it."

Dave said nothing.

"In fact," Gove went on gently, "you'd be doing us a kindness to ride out of this country and forget us. We've broken the law, technically, to try and spare a fine girl."

Beth said coldly to Dave, "If you ram around here the way you have been everybody will know."

Dave came to his feet then and stepped over and laid the paper on the desk. He wanted to get out of here and quickly. This was all too glib, and he felt a hot contempt for Beth

Hilliard for believing it.

He looked at her and found her watching him. "Are you satisfied?" she asked.

Dave nodded and turned toward the door.

Beth said, "You lost your horse, didn't you? I'll have them get you another."

Dave opened the door, nodded to Gove, and let Beth go ahead of him, shutting the door afterward.

They walked in silence toward the bunkhouse. Pete Framm was sitting in the doorway of it, and Beth, as they approached him, said, "Will you saddle up my buckskin for Mr. Wallace, Pete?"

Pete headed for the corral, and as soon as Beth was past the bunkhouse she slowed her pace.

She looked obliquely at Dave and then said, "Do you think an untrustworthy man would have been that considerate to a rustler's wife?"

A hard caution had held Dave's face expressionless so far: he wanted a horse with which to get out of here. But Beth Hilliard's words angered him beyond caution, prodding him into a protest that he spoke in a sardonic, suppressed anger. "He was considerate of Mrs. Macy, all right. Only that don't count a damn."

Beth was shocked into a moment's silence by his vehemence. "Then what does count?"

"A man's dead, killed," Dave said grimly. "Do

106

you keep it quiet to save his wife, or do you turn over a whole country to find out who killed him?"

"But if Tip was rustling he deserved what he got!"

"With Gove and Chance the judge of whether he deserved it!" Dave said angrily.

"They don't judge it! Everyone knows what happens to cattle thieves."

"If he was a cattle thief," Dave countered.

He and Beth stared angrily at each other for a moment, and then Dave left her, cutting over to the downed Chevron horse. He'd said enough, too much. But Beth Hilliard was blinded by her loyalty to Gove. Didn't she think it strange that Seegrist would risk killing him there on the desert? Or that Chance was out to finish him when she walked in here an hour ago?

He unloosened the cinch of the saddle on the dead horse and tugged the stirrup free, his face dark and scowling. When he had taken off the bridle, too, he turned toward the corral and discovered that Beth Hilliard had followed him and was waiting for him.

As she turned toward the corral with him she said coldly, "I'm sorry about the welcome you got here. But it's not wise to beat up one of our hands twice and then ride into the place on a horse you've taken from him."

Dave said nothing. His jaw was set grimly,

his face unfriendly and coldly hostile. Seeing it, Beth said no more. Pete Framm led out a long-legged buckskin gelding, and Beth, smiling, went up to the horse and stroked his nose.

Dave saddled him while Pete, quiet and expert, slipped the bridle on.

As Dave was ready to step into the saddle Beth Hilliard said, "Leave him with Sam and tell him to sell him. On my account, if he's sold."

Dave looked at her, and his face said plainly that he didn't understand.

"Sam Kinsley, the sheriff in Vermillion," Beth said. Close thunder seem to carom off the peaks now, and a cold wind whipped a strand of her hair across her face. She brushed it back and waited until the thunder died and then explained in a matter-of-fact voice, "I'm selling my share of Chevron to Jess. Sam has some Chevron horses from the reservation he's selling for us. This horse is not one of them; this is mine. He's to credit me with the sale, instead of the company. Is that clear?"

Dave nodded.

Beth said, "My buckskin ought to be a passport out of this country. If I were you I'd leave."

Dave stepped into the saddle and said, "Thanks," and Beth turned back for the house without a word of parting.

Dave, watching her briefly, saw her look up at the clouds bringing the coming rain and then look down again. He was aware that young Pete Framm was watching him as he still held the bridle.

Dave smiled and said, "Obliged."

Pete said softly, "Arnie Chance drifted out while you were in the house."

Dave regarded him silently, aware that Pete was trying to tell him something, liking the brash, reckless look of him.

"Kinsley?" Dave murmured.

Pete shook his head in negation. "You better keep to the brush."

Dave nodded once, slowly, and said, "Oh." He lowered the hand that held the reins and rested the butt of his palm on the saddle horn. "You're riding in some pretty cold company, Pete."

"They haven't spooked you yet," Pete pointed out, and added, "It's the other way around. You've got Seegrist so scared he wants to drift."

"He'll drift," Dave said quietly. He lifted the reins. "When you want to quit, Pete, look up Ives." He touched spurs to his horse, and Pete said abruptly:

"Hold on a minute." Color crept into his tanned face, but he said doggedly, "I want to ask you a question. This Mrs.

Macy. Did you come for her?"

"To see her."

"Not take her?"

"No."

Pete grinned, then, and stepped back and raised a hand in quiet salute. A blast of thunder shook the very earth as Dave rode out to the nearest timber.

It was after dark, and old Ives sprawled comfortably under his slanting ground sheet on which the rain was dripping. He'd let the fire die into coals, and they sizzled softly as the few drops of rain which succeeded in sifting through the thick spruce above hit them. He had been busy today after his own fashion. He'd brought his other horse over from the mountain pasture where he'd been grazing and had bought some grub in Hilliard, as he had promised Dave Wallace he would. Afterward he'd rounded up a Dutch oven, a ground sheet, a change of clothes, and such, that transformed this camp into something permanent. Later he got down to business, which was circling Hilliard and reading the comings and goings of the slope in the tracks left in the wagon road. This road was Ives's newspaper; in its dirt he read everything that was necessary for him to know, and out of today's reading he had gleaned one mildly significant fact. Sheriff Sam Kinsley had drifted into Hilliard from Vermillion after the rain started.

Ives raised his head now and listened, and when he was sure of it he came to his knees and threw a dry pitch knot and a couple of sticks of wood on the fire.

Presently he looked up from the fire and saw Dave Wallace, his slicker and hat channeling water, ride into the circle of firelight and pull up. There was no welcome on Dave's sober face.

"I'll bum one more feed from you," Dave said without friendliness.

"Light and eat," Ives invited.

The big man dismounted, and Ives noticed now that he was riding Beth Hilliard's buckskin. Dave came over to the fire, shucked out of his slicker, and sat down under the slanting tarp. Ives silently raked the Dutch oven and an oversize battered coffeepot from the coals and placed them beside Wallace. Ives was careful not to talk, because he could sense the big man's pride. After what had passed between them this morning only his hunger had driven him here, not an affection for Ives, and Ives knew it. This would have to be handled with infinite delicacy, if he were to succeed, Ives judged.

First he let Dave fill himself. Dave wiped out the Dutch oven with a handful of grass, emptied the coffeepot, and then leaned back and rolled a smoke and lighted it. His face was somber, preoccupied. Legs crossed tailor fashion, he stared at the fire a long time, and Ives watched him patiently.

"Well, you were right. I missed my chance," Dave said presently.

Ives wisely refrained from commenting. He only said, almost with indifference, "So you're headin' back now."

Dave turned to regard him with a cool, level stare. "Did I say I was?"

"What are you waitin' for?"

"To see Mrs. Macy."

"Well, why don't you?" Ives asked mildly.

Wallace told him, then, what he'd done this day. He took it from Hyam saying that Gove and Beth and Mrs. Macy had gone to Chevron to his fight at Chevron. Ives listened with a mute and bewildered astonishment at the account of the fight. Dave told him everything, emphasizing Gove's explanation of Tip Macy's death. He also told him that both Gove and Beth had warned him to leave the country. But, stubborn still, he had ridden over to Pitchfork to find Mrs. Macy and had learned that Arnie Chance had been a half-hour ahead of him and had taken Martha Macy back to Chevron. So at every step, Dave said, they were ahead of him. Gove had covered himself to Beth, and he had ordered Dave to leave the country.

When he was finished Ives sat there in silence, turning all this over in his mind. Something, he was certain now, was terribly wrong at Chevron. It made him more determined than ever to keep Wallace here.

"So you'll stick, anyway?" Ives asked mildly.

"Till I see her," Dave repeated.

Ives nodded toward the horse. "Then you better get rid of that horse."

Dave tossed his cigarette away. "I don't give a damn if they know I've got him. I'm going to buy him because I'll need him."

"She won't sell him."

"She will. She's selling him."

Ives looked at him curiously. "Who said?" he asked skeptically.

"She's selling Chevron and everything with it," Dave said indifferently.

Ives was still just one second, and then he boiled to his knees and grabbed Dave's arm and savagely yanked him around. "What did you say?"

Dave said wonderingly, "She's selling Chevron."

"Who to?"

"Gove."

Ives's hand slowly fell away, and he stared at Dave and then rose and stood out in the rain, staring at the fire.

This was it. This was the reason for the change in Gove and Chance. Without knowing how or why this was so, Ives was dead certain that this was it. His mind hurdled reasons and methods and arrived at one point only — wanting Chevron was behind the change in Gove.

He said suddenly, "She ain't sold yet?"

"No."

Ives reached under the tarp and drew Dave's slicker to him.

"Listen, Wallace," Ives said mildly. "I'm leavin' now. I'll be back in a couple of hours. If you ain't still here when I get back I'm goin' to track you down if it takes ten years, because I need you, and you need me. Will you wait?"

"Why should I?" Dave said, still not friendly.

"Damn you, you stay here," Ives said and went out into the night for his horse.

He got his mare and rode out in the wet night. The bleak skepticism that old Ives lived by served him in good stead now. He'd been expecting something, had sensed it, just as Con Buckley had, and now it was here. And he had a pretty good idea what he was going to do and he didn't bother to explain why to himself. Part of the reason, of course, was his friendship for dead Joe Hilliard, but the most of it was Beth. He had a proprietary interest in her. Hadn't he shown her her first beaver, taught her to ride Indian fashion, discussed her first beaux with her? Hadn't she asked him if she should marry

114

Sam Kinsley, who loved her? Above all, when she'd wanted to leave her father and Chevron to have a look at the world and see what she was made of, hadn't she talked to him about it even before she told her father she was leaving for the East to teach school? She was Ives's whole family and his love and his burden, and something was happening to her.

The chill drizzle continued, turning into a raw rain when he reached the wagon road that wasn't sheltered by timber. When he came to the slippery grade that led down into Hilliard he reined up, looking at the few lights below.

Afterward he descended and left his horse at the stable and tramped up the muddy street in the rain. The lights of the hotel and the Olympus were reflected again and again in the water pooling the rutted street.

Ives made his way hurriedly, certain as to his first move. He felt Con would agree.

· He stepped into the Olympus, stamping the mud from his moccasins, and looked around him. The hostler, his slicker still dripping, was having something warm at the bar with a couple of Star 33 riders. Hyam, the hotel-keeper, was playing a game of double solitaire at a back table, a bottle on the table before him. But it was the man opposite Hyam that Ives settled his attention on. Sheriff Sam Kinsley was tilted back against the wall, his feet on the

115

rungs of his chair, a ragged newspaper held up in front of him.

Ives reflected a short moment, and then he knew what he was going to do. He shucked out of his slicker and went back to Hyam's table. The hotelkeeper looked up and nodded, and Ives ignored him. He slipped into a chair and said to Sam Kinsley, "Hello, Sam."

Kinsley's paper came down immediately. On his heavy face was a look of mild pleasure as he said, "Long time no see, Ives."

Ives shook his hand and then said bluntly, "I hear Beth Hilliard has sold out her share of Chevron."

A look of consternation came into Kinsley's face. He glanced at Hyam, who was listening, and then turned to see if the men at the bar had overheard Ives. They hadn't.

He said in a low voice, with considerable skepticism, "Who said so?"

Ives raised his voice and yelled to the bartender, "Gus, was it you told me Beth Hilliard had sold out her share of Chevron to Gove?"

The whole barroom knew now, which was what Ives intended. The source of his information would be impossible to trace now that everybody knew.

"Not me," the bartender said.

"Was it you?" Ives asked the hostler.

"Hunh-unh," the hostler replied.

116

"Didn't know it."

Ives looked at Sam. "I disremember who it was. But I heard."

There was a plain look of chagrin and exasperation on Kinsley's sober face, and Ives took a sly pleasure in it. Kinsley rose and said, "Come here, Ives," and went over to a far table where there was privacy.

Ives followed him and sat down, and Kinsley leaned his elbows on the table and said sullenly, "Do you have to shout it to the whole country?"

"What?"

"About Chevron."

"Is it a secret?"

"Not exactly," Kinsley growled. "Only Gove and Beth didn't want it spread."

"Nobody told me," Ives said flatly, grouchily. "How the hell do I know when folks want things told and when they don't? A man's going to have to get a license to listen here, pretty quick."

Kinsley sighed and shook his head. Like everyone else, he knew he couldn't argue with Ives unless he was prepared to hit him, and he couldn't do that. "All right, all right," he said wearily. "Let it go."

Ives said, "I wanted to talk to you about it."

"All right."

"Chevron owes me four hundred dollars'

bounty for twenty gray wolves I trapped on its lease. Who pays?"

"Why – Gove, I'd suppose," Kinsley said reluctantly.

Ives appeared thoughtful. This next had to be done in a delicate manner, in order to make it look real.

"Chevron had a mighty tough winter, didn't it?" Ives asked.

"They were wiped out."

Ives rubbed his chin musingly. "Well, a tough winter means damn little money. And I reckon Gove is using all he has to buy out Beth. Maybe I better forget my bounty money."

A look of gratefulness crept into Kinsley's face. Ives knew, as did the whole slope, that Sam Kinsley was Jess Gove's friend. Of all the people who honored Jess Gove's gray hairs, his gentle ways, his generosity, none honored them in quite the manner of Kinsley. It was with a mixture of humility, worship, and privilege. He would have liked Gove if only because Gove was a partner of Beth Hilliard. To Kinsley, no sane man would ask more of this world than to be the husband of Beth Hilliard and the friend of Jess Gove. And since the one was lacking he made up for it by coveting the other.

Kinsley said slowly, "Well, it would help, Ives. But you earned the money."

Ives scratched his head in feigned perplexity.

"Don't get me wrong," he said in his irascible voice. "I ain't a buzzard. On the other hand, I got my rights. If Gove's got money enough to buy Chevron, he might have money enough to pay me. On the other hand, I wouldn't want my claim to stop him."

"But it would," Kinsley said quietly.

Ives was immediately skeptical. "He tell you?"

Kinsley hunched forward in his chair. "This is strictly between us, Ives. You understand?"

"It is, so far," Ives said dryly.

"Gove hasn't got any money," Kinsley said. "He was wiped out this winter. He had all his savings invested in that Texas herd that was winterkilled. Two thousand head."

"Then how's he buyin' out Beth?"

"Borrowing."

"Then why can't he pay me?" Ives asked truculently, "I'll take a bank's money any day."

"Hear the rest of it," Kinsley said seriously. "Gove isn't borrowing from any bank, and he hasn't any backer, Ives. Every man with money in this country is waiting until the Chevron grass money falls due in a couple of weeks. They know Gove hasn't the money to pay for the Ute lease, and they also know if he can't pay, then the lease will be thrown open to the highest bidder. So why should they loan Gove money, when they can take the same money and lease the grass that Chevron used to have?"

"You mean Gove ain't goin' to keep the lease?"

"He can't. He hasn't the money to pay for it."

Ives scowled. "Then what the hell is he buyin' from 'Beth?"

"Chevron."

"But there ain't any graze there. That's just a pretty house set on a pasture."

Kinsley nodded. "That's it. That's all Gove wants. Just a place to keep him alive until he dies."

Ives was silent. He was thinking of Con Buckley and how Con offered to loan Gove money and was coldly turned away. And now Gove was claiming he couldn't borrow the money to pay the grass lease.

"Who's he borrowin' from then?" Ives said bluntly.

"A friend."

"You," Ives said.

Kinsley hesitated and then nodded reluctantly.

Ives said in his cantankerous way, "I got a right to know how much, ain't I?"

"A thousand," Kinsley said. "Because without the reservation graze, Chevron is just a postage-stamp spread or a line camp. Bell, over at Pitchfork, offered three hundred for the house to use as a line camp, so you see what it's worth. Jess set a reasonable price at fifteen hundred, and Beth agreed. Beth's two-thirds share of the Dun River Cattle Company would come to a thousand then, and I loaned it to Jess."

"And the company dissolves?"

"It's all Jess'. It won't do him any good, but he'd like to keep it going for reasons of sentiment." Kinsley paused then and looked at Ives and shook his head and made a wry face. "Beth wants to go back East. It'll give her a little money and give Jess a home till he dies. I guess that's all that's left of Joe Hilliard's Dun River Cattle Company, Ives."

Ives nodded. He felt a terrible urgency within him, but he didn't move. He seemed to be thinking, and presently he asked, "When does it change hands?"

"Day after tomorrow morning. Rollins over at the store is a notary, and I'll be a witness."

That was all Ives wanted to know. He sat a moment longer, then stood up. He said harshly, "You tell Gove to hell with the bounty money. He can pay me whenever he wants to."

Kinsley rose now, smiling in his slow, heavy way. "That's kind of you, Ives. Mighty kind."

Ives was afraid to look at him, for fear he would say what was in his mind. He merely waved his hand in a deprecatory gesture.

"Keep it to yourself," Kinsley said.

Ives stopped and looked at him. "You said that once."

Kinsley sighed. Ives's moment of reasonableness, of generosity, was past, and Kinsley supposed he couldn't expect more. He said mildly, "So I did," and walked back to his newspaper.

Ives chatted a moment with the hostler at the bar and then went back to Con's office. He went in without bothering to knock, closed the door behind him, and before Con Buckley could turn around to greet him Ives asked, "How much money can you get hold of and in how short a time without a damn person knowin' it?"

Fat Con Buckley didn't move. He seemed to be staring at his desk, and Ives sat down. Presently Con turned to him and said, "Fifteen thousand in a week or ten days."

"How much can you lay your hands on now?"

"Five thousand."

"Give it here," Ives said.

When Ives reached camp, Wallace was still there. The rain had stopped, and Ives staked his horse out and came back to camp.

He approached the tarp and threw a heavy sack of coins on the blanket and peeled out of his slicker.

Wallace eyed him suspiciously while he stoked the fire. Ives knelt there, holding his cold hands over the mounting blaze.

He looked up at Wallace then and said quietly, "How bad do you want to find out about Tip Macy?"

"Bad," Wallace said slowly.

"I'll make a deal with you."

When Dave frowned Ives said quietly, "I want somethin' bad, too, Wallace. I want to find out why Beth Hilliard is sellin' Chevron. I want to find out so bad that I aim to buy Chevron to keep Gove from gettin' it."

Dave said nothing.

"The deal is this. You buy Chevron with the money I give you. You help Beth Hilliard every way I tell you. Do that and I'll find out how Tip Macy died."

"No," Dave said flatly.

Ives scowled. "Why not? It's a fair trade. Any move you make toward Martha Macy, Gove nails you. I can talk to her any time. Any move I make toward helpin' Beth, Gove stands ready to stop me."

"No," Dave repeated.

"What's wrong with it?"

"One thing," Wallace said quietly. "I don't like Beth Hilliard. I wouldn't help her."

"Why not?" Ives asked blankly.

"I don't like her. She's a fool girl, not worth anybody's help."

Ives rose slowly, his face suddenly gone

white. "I ought to kill you for that," he said quietly.

"You asked me. You found out," Wallace said bluntly.

Ives got a grip on himself. This wasn't the way to do it. Beyond that, he could even see some justice in Wallace thinking what he did.

"Listen," Ives said sourly, truculently. "You don't have to like her. I don't like you, but that won't stop us from makin' a trade. Think, man, think! This is a business deal. We can use each other."

Wallace said nothing, but there was a small doubt in his eyes now.

Ives said, "As long as you shut up about Macy, you're free to move around this country. And I can find out about Macy for you."

Still Dave said nothing.

"You trust me?" Ives asked.

Dave nodded.

"And I trust you," Ives said bluntly. "I'm only asking for a word as good as the word I give. I can help you. I can find out about Macy."

Reluctantly, after a long pause, Dave said, "All right, I'll help her."

"Just one thing," Ives said soberly. "Whatever you think about that girl, you keep it to yourself." He put out his hand. "Agreed?"

As Dave shook hands with him Ives said truculently, "You damn well better mean that, because I do. Now you listen while I talk."

And far into the night he did.

CHAPTER 7

Tom Hyam regarded his freshly shaven face in the wavy-surfaced mirror and whistled thinly in exclamation, then grimaced and turned away. His eyes were bloodshot, the pouches under them an almost purple color. He shrugged into a clean, pleated-bosom shirt, and tied his string tie and stepped out into the hotel corridor, shrugging into his coat. He wondered idly if he had such a hard head for liquor after all. Even after sleeping into the afternoon he felt drugged, thick, unclean.

Downstairs the latest of the lunchers had left the dining room, and the fourteen-year-old daughter of the Mexican cook was clearing table.

Hyam said, "Mrs. Macy come back yet?"

At the girl's negative Hyam went out through the lobby, picking up his hat on the desk as he passed, and went out. The bright midafternoon sunshine hurt his eyes, but he sniffed appreciatively of the warm, washed air after the night's rain. The wagons this morning had churned up the black mud of the street, and Hyam clung to the boardwalk. Passing across from the Olympus, dead in the drowsy heat, he gave the saloon a baleful glance and went on.

At the feed stable he rented a saddle horse, mounted, and rode north out of town, over the bridge.

It was good to get air in his lungs once more instead of alcohol fumes. He listened to the afternoon stillness with pleasure and then hung his black Stetson over the saddle horn, letting the sun burn his face and neck. He rode with an expertness that was almost incongruous with his black dandified gambler's clothes.

Later he rolled and smoked a cigarette, passing up the long black cheroots which jutted up from his coat pocket. He judged that now was the time to make his first move. For a month now he'd been studiously offensive to everyone, had been drunk too much of the time to suit himself, and had made himself thoroughly unliked. With that as a foundation, what was to follow at Chevron could be reasonably simple if things broke right. For Hyam had observed that Gove wanted Mrs. Macy kept away from people, and Hyam was going to demand that she return to work. By giving in gracefully when Gove demurred he might strike up the acquaintance that was so necessary.

Four miles above Hilliard he put his horse

onto the timbered grade where the road clung to the river and pulled his feet from the stirrups, luxuriously stretching his legs. The sun was hot, and he yawned.

And then he heard the shot – a rifle shot, sharp and flat in the still afternoon.

It came from around the bend in the road ahead and seemed close. He yanked his horse around and put him into the Little Dun and was almost across the stream when three shots, in quick succession, slapped out, as if in answer to the first. Those were from a six-gun, Hyam noted behind thought.

He put his horse into the brush and up the timbered slope, and above the crashing of his horse he heard some shouting. When the going got too steep Hyam slipped from the saddle, quickly wrapped his reins around a tree, looked back and down toward the river and couldn't see it, and then climbed on afoot, knowing his horse was hidden.

At the top of the sharp hog's-back he bellied down and crawled to the ridge and studied the canyon below. It was wide, and he could see the road and the river bending around the curve. There was a horse downed on the wagon road, and it had pinned a man beneath it. This man was not fighting to get out from under. And crossing the stream, hatless, gun in hand, was Jess Gove. His horse splashed the river water head-high as he ran.

Hyam watched Gove take the slope of the hill, hunting in diagonals, like a pointer dog, pushing his magnificent black to its utmost, climbing the hill, and beating the brush.

And then Hyam saw something that narrowed his attention swiftly, made him hold his breath.

The slope was covered with short scrub oak below thick pine saplings. There at the edge of the saplings and lying sprawled in the scrub oak was the lower half of the body of a man. He noticed it because Gove rode right past it and plunged into the saplings. The man in the scrub oak rolled aside a little to let Gove pass. Within two minutes Gove's horse came out of the saplings, again past the man. And this time Hyam saw the hidden man's hand raise a little in salute, which Gove saw but ignored on his way down the slope.

Gove hit the river, crossed it, and dismounted by the downed horse. Then he dallied a rope around the saddle of the downed horse, mounted his own black, and put him into the river again. Then he took up the slack in the rope, and his black slowly dragged the downed horse off the rider.

Gove came back, dismounted, and knelt beside the downed man. Hyam could see now that it was Seegrist. Gove examined him and then knelt there, motionless, as if making up his mind.

Then he picked up Seegrist and laid him gently across the black's saddle. Gove swung up behind him, then picked up Seegrist and managed to seat him in the saddle. Holding him upright with his free arm around him, Gove rode off and was soon out of sight around the bend toward Hilliard.

Hyam's attention shifted now to the man who was hidden. Gove and Seegrist were barely out of sight when the man came to his knees, then to his feet.

The man, Hyam saw, was Arnie Chance.

Hyam watched Chance fade into the timber, and presently, from over the second ridge, he caught the sound of a horse moving through the brush. Finally it was silent.

Hyam came to his feet and brushed off his clothes and turned back downhill, picking his way carefully. He was not so much surprised as he was puzzled at what he had just witnessed. On the face of it, it didn't make sense. The foreman of Chevron knocking over the horse of a Chevron hand who was riding with the Chevron owner.

That might be explained, but what followed — Gove passing within a few feet of Chance and refusing to see him — pointed to the fact that Gove wanted this and had planned it.

Hyam couldn't pretend to furnish a reason, and it baffled him.

He put his horse back on the wagon road and when he came to Seegrist's downed horse he observed him carefully. The shot had missed Seegrist's knee by inches and had caught the horse squarely behind the shoulder in the heart. There was no mistake here; Chance hadn't wanted to shoot Seegrist; he'd wanted to scare him.

Hyam sat there, weighing his next move. Gove was the one he wanted to see, and Gove had ridden on to Hilliard. Still, there had to be a start to this, and now he had a double justification for his visit.

He rode into Chevron in late afternoon. Pete Framm, who had the spring wagon up on blocks and was greasing the wheels by the wagon shed, saw him first and left the barn at a swift walk to intercept him.

Hyam reined up, and when he saw Pete he remembered him. He saw, too, by the truculent look on Pete's young face that he also remembered their meeting in the hotel.

Hyam said, "I'm looking for Mrs. Macy."

"What for?" Pete demanded.

"She's supposed to be working for me," Hyam said. "Either she does or she doesn't. I'd like to know which."

Pete bent down and yanked out a handful of

grass and carefully wiped the grease from his hands. Then he looked full at Hyam and said, "It's a damn shame, the people a woman has to work for, ain't it?"

Hyam said quietly, "Careful, my friend, or she won't have a job."

"She ain't got a real one now," Pete said flatly. "If you fire her for what I think about you I'm goin' to give myself the pleasure of unscrewin' your head and hidin' it."

Hyam sneered. "Maybe you'd find that work."

"Any time you want to find out, just climb off. Or you want me to climb up?"

Hyam pulled a thin cigar from his breast pocket and lighted it. He looked more dissolute than ever as he rolled the cigar to the corner of his mouth and squinted against the smoke. "Any other time it would be a pleasure. Right now I've got business."

"I wouldn't call it urgent business," Pete taunted. "Just step down."

"Maybe Miss Hilliard would," Hyam murmured. "There's a Chevron horse down the road, still saddled, with a bullet through its heart."

Pete looked carefully at him, and his face altered. He said swiftly, "What kind of horse?"

"Bay. Double-rig saddle. Lots of hardware on the bridle."

Pete's mouth opened a little, then he turned and strode toward the house. Hyam walked his horse behind him. Pete knocked at the door of the office and went in. Presently Beth Hilliard came out, wearing a man's blue jeans and checked shirt. Pete Framm trailed her.

She came up to Hyam, distress in her face, and nodded civilly. "What about this horse?" she asked.

Hyam repeated the description, and Beth said immediately, "That's Ed Seegrist's horse."

She looked at Pete for confirmation, and he nodded, and then she looked back at Hyam. "Was there — was Ed shot?"

"I don't think so. I didn't look carefully."

"Dave Wallace," Beth murmured almost inaudibly.

"Maybe not," Pete said. "Maybe this tinhorn shoots horses for fun."

"Pete!" Beth said.

"That's all right! We're old friends," Pete drawled, looking at Hyam. "I'm just tryin' to get a knife through that hide of his."

"Go saddle my horse," Beth said peremptorily. "Saddle your own too."

Pete nodded, looked once more at Hyam, and headed for the corral.

Beth said, "I must apologize for him."

"We don't exactly like each other since he tried to annoy my hotel help," Hyam said

133

calmly. "Matter of fact, that's why I rode up. Is Mrs. Macy still working for me?"

"No," Beth said. "It was kind of you to give her the job. But she's staying with us. Now, will you show us where Seegrist's horse is?"

"A pleasure," Hyam said courteously.

In a few minutes Beth, Hyam and Pete rode off the place.

From the thick timber on the west side of the meadow old Ives and Dave Wallace watched them ride out, and Dave said, "She's alone now."

Ives came to his feet and said, "Remember, it's that windfall just beyond the house. Put yourself behind the tree closest to it. I'll give you ten minutes."

Dave went back to his horse and rode around the open pasture, keeping well into the timber. When the rampart of rock that jutted up above the timber lay in the right direction he dismounted and carefully worked his way to the edge of the meadow. Presently he saw the windfall Ives spoke of. It was a thick pine and lay angling out into the grass, its branches long since lopped off, its trunk rotting.

He worked down to a tall jack pine on the edge of the pasture and hunkered down behind it, waiting.

Ives gave him ten minutes, then circled around and picked up the trail from Pitchfork that came out into the clearing behind the barn.

He walked his mare down it, and when he came out in the open two of the crew squatting down against the log barn saw him. Ives pulled in toward them, and the oldest one rose. He was Ray and he had worked for Chevron almost since Ives could remember, content with his meager pay for a lazy man's work.

"Beth home, Ray?" Ives asked.

"Nope. Just left."

Ives looked at the house and saw smoke issuing from the chimney.

"You're lyin'," Ives said flatly. He put his horse in motion and headed for the house. Ray looked at the other puncher and shook his head and grinned. The younger man came to his feet, and they both watched Ives.

He headed for the kitchen wing of the house and rode up to the door. He came so close that he had only to lean out of the saddle and rap sharply on the door.

It opened, and Martha Macy stood there. Ives had known her since she was a child and had paid her no attention, since she was no kin of Joe Hilliard. Martha recognized Ives too. It was evident in her small face, on which there was no sign of welcome, only recognition. She looked tired and scared, Ives thought.

He knew Ray and the other hand were watching, and he had to make this short.

He said quietly, "You want to find out who murdered Tip?"

Martha Macy looked as if she'd been hit. She stepped back a little, and Ives thought she was going to faint. Ives knew there was a brutal shock in the question, and it was what he wanted. Before Martha could frame an answer Ives said, "In about fifteen minutes or so go out and sit on the windfall close to the timber past the rocks. Tell 'em you're goin' for a walk." He rode off then, crossing the bridge on his way to the wagon road.

Martha stood in the doorway watching him. When her moment of unbelief was past she thought she hadn't heard rightly. How did Ives know Tip had been murdered? And what did his question mean, since if he already knew Tip was murdered, then he also knew why he'd been killed? Panic was on her. The thing she'd been dreading and hating for these long months was here. The news was out, if Ives knew about it.

She turned away from the door and went over to the big kitchen table and sat down in one of its chairs. She stared absently at the big stove and then the sink and then the clock, and her mind refused to work; her eyes refused to see. The shame was here, and from now on she'd have to face it. What she'd been doing —

slaving at hard jobs and relying solely on Gove to shield her — would be a pleasure in comparison with what was coming. For she had a personal devil, and it was pride. And it was breaking her.

Just so long as people believed Tip died doing his job, she could bear his loss and her misfortune. But when they knew he'd been killed in a sordid cattle-stealing deal she couldn't face them. She thought bleakly of the dances before her family died, before she was married, when men invited each other out into the night to fight over her favor. She could have married any man on this slope, rich or poor, and she'd chosen Tip against the advice of all her friends. To admit that Tip was rustling and was shot for it was to admit that she'd made a mistake, that she'd been a headstrong fool and had been swindled by a cheap thief. And she couldn't do it, wouldn't do it.

She rose suddenly, a kind of wildness in her. How far had this gone, and how did Ives know? She had to find out and stop it. She knew behind thought that she was being selfish and almost shoddy in her frantic determination that nobody should know how Tip died, but she could no more help herself than she could stop breathing. Crossing to the door, she slipped into an old coat hanging on a nail behind it and stepped out into the dusk. The sun was gone, and it was immediately cool.

The crew was washing up at the bench in front of the cookshack. She strolled toward the front of the house in full sight of them. Chance would have told them to keep an eye on her, but he wasn't here. Since Dave Wallace's coming Gove had tried to protect her in every way possible, and he had asked her to help him.

Ray eyed her, and she stopped and looked at the valley. Presently, folding her arms across her breast, she strolled on across the meadow, pausing now and then to look at the evening. Ray was watching her, undecided as to whether he should warn her. But her pace, the way she loitered, disarmed him.

She was close to the timber now, and she kept watching it for any sign of life and saw none. When she came to the windfall she chose a spot nearest the timber and sat down. Ramming her hands in her coat pocket, she put her legs out straight before her and waited, her excitement almost unbearable.

When the voice came it was close enough to startle her.

"I'm Tip's friend, Dave Wallace."

Martha knew then that she'd been trapped, that Ives had decoyed her out here to talk to the very man whom Gove said could do the most harm.

She came to her feet, still facing the meadow,

and Dave Wallace's voice came sharply, "Sit down! I know who murdered Tip. I want help."

Martha said coldly. "Who told you?"

"Gove."

For a moment Martha was speechless. "You're lying," she said.

"He was found at the boundary-line camp with a forged bill of sale in his pocket."

Martha sank back on the log now, a sudden bewilderment keeping her silent.

Dave Wallace said quietly. "Gove told me. Yet he won't let me see you because he's afraid I'll make you tell me the same thing. Does that make sense?"

"No," Martha said in a small voice. She couldn't see Dave Wallace, could only remember the way Tip had spoken of him, yet she had a picture of him that his voice bore out. A quiet, slow-spoken big man with a kind of taciturn face and a sharp, seldom-seen humor.

"You can help me," Dave Wallace said.

"I — can't," Martha answered weakly. "That's all I know."

"You're wrong. If you didn't know more Gove wouldn't care if I saw you."

Martha didn't answer.

And then when Wallace spoke again his voice was almost gentle. "You've been ashamed of Tip, haven't you? Without ever being sure he was stealing cattle."

"Gove said he was!" Martha replied swiftly. "The forged bill of sale proved it!"

Dave answered quietly, "Anybody could have forged that bill of sale and put it in Tip's pocket. That's the only proof Gove's got, and he's afraid to show it to the sheriff. How good is it, then — or have you thought of that?"

Martha didn't answer, and Dave said into the falling darkness, "Gove lied all the way along. Tip never stole a cow in his life. I'd stake my neck on it and I'm going to."

Martha was glad then that she wasn't face to face with Dave Wallace. That quiet certainty with which he'd said this brought the color to her face and shame to her heart. In the months since Tip's death she had even put her humiliation at his crime ahead of her doubt of his guilt. And now she felt both a deep disgust and a new hope.

She said miserably, "How can I help?"

"Sit there and look at the house and tell me what happened. Tell me the exact words. Because you said something to someone that scared Gove. He's afraid you'll say it again. Start from Tip's death. Take it up through every talk with Gove. Talk fast, because it's getting dark."

Martha was quiet a moment, thinking. She'd gone over this a hundred nights, remembering it until it hurt so much she thought she'd go crazy. She could remember it letter perfect, and she began in a swift, low voice, "It was the afternoon following the day of the blizzard. It was snowing hard still. I saw a rider heading for the brush shed outside of our shack and I thought it was Tip. I put a coat on and was halfway out in the storm when I saw it was Arnie Chance. I could tell something was wrong when he stepped in. 'What is it, Arnie?' I asked. He couldn't look at me. He fumbled with his hat and then blurted out, 'I reckon there's no easy way to tell you, Mrs. Macy. Tip got caught in the blizzard. It got him.' I don't remember what I did then. What I remember next was sitting on the edge of the bed and Chance was watching me. I said, 'I want to see him,' and he said, 'You can't. There'll be five feet of snow at the boundary-line camp by tonight,' and I said, 'But not half that much where Tip is,' and he said, 'That's where he is,' and I said, 'I guess —'"

Dave said swiftly, "What did you mean, 'Not half that much where Tip is'?"

Martha said, "When Tip left he said he was heading for the Seco line camp. That's close to the Rim."

"And where's the boundary-line camp?"

"High up, south, on the edge of the reservation."

Dave was silent so long that Martha won-

141

dered if he was still there. At last she said, "Does that mean anything, Dave?"

"That's it," Dave answered softly.

"But what —?"

"I don't know," Dave cut in. "That's all I want, though. You go back to the house. Walk slow. Come back here at the same time night after next. If you tell anybody, even Beth Hilliard, about me or Ives, it'll mean a bullet in my back. Ives' too. You understand?"

Martha shivered, and it was not from the evening chill.

"Dave."

"Yes?"

"I'll make this up to Tip! I'll make it up someway! I've got to!"

"Sure you will," Dave said gently. "Now go back."

It was only when she was down in the meadow again that she realized she hadn't even seen Dave Wallace. It didn't matter.

CHAPTER 8

It was a combination of things that made Beth dread the sight of Hilliard next morning. The chiefest reason was the one she refused to think about; in another hour or so she would no longer be a part of Chevron. Then there was Ed Seegrist, in bed in the hotel with what had seemed to be a badly crushed chest from his fall yesterday when his horse was shot under him. But beyond that there was Sam Kinsley waiting for her — Sam, whose doglike, devoted eyes were still beseeching after two years. She had put off seeing him alone in Vermillion the morning after she got in, when she and Jess had discussed with him the wisdom of her selling her share of Chevron. But she could not evade him forever, and Sam was not the kind of man to wait for the time and place to propose to her again. He had a headlong stubborn way about him that almost frightened her. And thinking of Sam, she thought of Ives, who had not been to see her. That troubled and hurt her, for she had needed Ives's advice these past days, and he had failed her.

Because this day was ceremonial she and Jess had come down in the buggy. Before they reached the bridge Beth drew a deep breath and said, "Let me out at the hotel, Jess. I'll see Ed first."

"I'll bring Rollins up there," Jess said.

He pulled up the team at the steep steps in front of the hotel and handed Beth down. Before she had climbed three steps Sam Kinsley, freshly shaven so that his square face was flushed pink and smelling of bay rum, was waiting for her, hat in hand.

She greeted him, and afterward Sam said heavily, "This is a sad day, Beth. I wish I could help."

"Sad?" Beth asked, and she was surprised at the tartness in her voice. "It's not sad, Sam. It's just sense. You said so yourself. Chevron will support one person, and since I'm a lone woman it can hardly be me."

She realized, with dismay, that she had paved the way in the first minute of conversation for Sam's inevitable question.

Before he could answer, then, she said quickly, "I want to see Ed, Sam."

"Certainly," Sam said.

She went into the lobby, and Sam followed her, his eyes openly admiring. In her blue dress that seemed to touch off the sheen of her chestnut hair she was tall and proud and everything a man would want. Sam Kinsley's jaw set a little in determination as he followed her up the steps to Seegrist's room.

Beth wasn't prepared for the sight that met her as she stepped into the darkened room. Ed's face was a dirty gray color, and his hands that plucked the covers seemed frail and weak. She had liked Ed Seegrist the least of any of the men who worked for Chevron, but now her heart was full of pity. There was fear in his eyes, fear of death, and she saw it as plainly as if he had said it.

She came to the bedside, stilling the revulsion she couldn't help but feel.

"How are you, Ed?"

Seegrist essayed a smile. His breathing rattled, as if there were something in his throat he couldn't clear. His voice was low, surprisingly strong when he spoke. "I feel broke in two, Miss Beth."

Beth sat down, reassured a little by the sound of his voice. "Should you talk, Ed?"

"That's all I can do."

Knowing the quiet ways of sympathy, Beth said, "Tell me about it, Ed."

"Nothin' to tell," Seegrist said bitterly. "Wallace just forted up on the slope by the second ford, and when I rode along with Jess he cut down on me."

145

"On your horse," Kinsley said quietly, for the sake of justice.

"On me," Seegrist said passionately. "The only reason I'm alive is because he ain't a good shot."

Beth looked at Sam, and he eyed her gravely. "Jess said he was still singing the same tune about Macy when he came to Chevron."

Beth nodded, for Jess had told her only to admit of Wallace's visit to Sam and nothing of what he'd said.

Sam looked at Seegrist and said, "He'll be taken care of, Ed, if he's still around. I think he shot your horse just to get even with Chevron before he left the country."

"He's crazy!" Seegrist whispered passionately. "I never seen him before in my life, and he tries to gun me."

"Are you sure you haven't, Ed?" Beth asked.

Seegrist just looked at her, and then his glance slid away. "Plumb sure."

Beth had the uncertain feeling that he wasn't telling the whole truth.

"Look, Miss Hilliard," Seegrist said. "I can't work for Chevron if he stays around here. He'll kill me!"

"He won't," Kinsley contradicted him. An edge of impatience was in his voice. "I told you, Ed, he's probably drifted out of the country. He wouldn't dare stay after this."

"You'll see," Seegrist whispered bitterly.

Beth stayed a moment longer, then rose, and she and Sam said good-by.

Downstairs Hyam was behind the small corner desk, writing something, and he greeted Beth courteously on her way to the veranda.

Sam pulled up a chair for her and she took it, and then he dragged one up beside her and sat down heavily.

Beth said, "How bad is Ed, Sam?"

"Pretty bad," Sam said soberly. "The horse rolled on him."

Beth was quiet a moment. "It's an odd man that will remember a grudge for five years."

"How five years?"

"Ed's been with us five years. Save for roundups and the drives across the reservation to the railroad, he's never been off the slope. And Wallace has never been here before. So their quarrel must have been before Ed came."

"Wallace is a plain hard case," Sam said grimly. Then he looked at Beth and said, "It's not your worry, Beth. You're finished with Chevron."

"I know."

' Sam pulled a cigar from his pocket and deliberately lighted it and then asked in a carefully neutral tone, "What are your plans, Beth?"

She had a feeling he was regarding her

searchingly, and she did not look at him. "Go back and teach school," she said.

"Why?" Sam demanded stubbornly. "Good God, a schoolteacher! That's all right. I've got nothing against the breed. But you're cut out for a – a –" he faltered.

"What, Sam?" Beth asked coldly.

Sam's heavy face flushed a little, and he threw his cigar away with a savage gesture and sat straighter in his chair. "Good lord, I've been writing this to you for two years. I don't know why I should be so shy about saying it. Beth, won't you marry me?"

"I wrote you I wouldn't, Sam."

It had come, as she knew it must, and for a moment she was almost angry. He had so little tact, so little sense of the fitness of things. It was all smothered beneath his heavy-handed messianic faith in his ability to change her mind, and she resented it deeply now.

"But you don't like it there," Sam said implacably. "Your letter said so."

"Perhaps I'll learn."

"But why leave here at all?" Sam demanded. "You're shut of Chevron. If you want to be a ranch wife I've got a ranch. If you want to be in town I'll sell the place. And I'll get ahead, Beth."

"I'm sure you will," Beth said quietly. "But you can't change my mind, Sam."

"But what's the matter with me?" Kinsley demanded doggedly. His eyes were hot and a little bit crazy, Beth thought. She was frightened. Here on a drowsy summer morning on a hotel porch in a town with people all around her, she was frightened of him. And it made her angry and hard.

"None of it concerns you, Sam," she said sharply. "You haven't a right to question me. I'm not your wife and I won't be, and you've got to understand it!"

She was standing when she finished, and Sam was too.

He looked at her as if she had hit him, and then he said bitterly, slowly, solemnly, "Beth, if I don't marry you no man will."

The sound of footsteps on the plank walk made Beth turn. There, coming up the steps, were Jess and Arthur Rollins, the storekeeper who was also the town's notary. Beth felt a wild relief at sight of them, and she stepped forward to greet Rollins, who seemed surprised by the warmth of her welcome.

Now it was sane again, and Beth felt herself drawing a quiet strength from Jess. He had not overheard them, for his seamed face was tranquil and grave. She put a hand on his arm and looked up at him and said, "Are we ready, Jess?"

Gove looked across at Kinsley and smiled. "If

Sam hasn't changed his mind, I reckon we are."

Beth didn't look at Sam. She took Gove's arm and walked into the lobby. Jess seated her at the table and then crossed to the desk to borrow pen and ink from Hyam. Beth chatted with Rollins while Sam stood sullenly beside her chair.

When the pen and ink were brought Jess took the deed from his pocket and unfolded it. It was short, and Beth read it through quickly and then reached for the pen.

Her hand was shaking a little, she noticed, and she took a deep breath and steadied it, awed a little by the irrevocability of what she was about to do. And then she put the pen to paper.

As she did so a voice drawled quietly into the room's stillness: "I'd wait a minute, Miss Hilliard."

Beth looked up at the sound of the voice and saw Dave Wallace standing there in the doorway. His big frame almost filled it, and there was something about his rough clothes, his scuffed half boots, and the way he was watching her, oblivious of the rest of them, that was almost a portent. She remembered Ed Seegrist upstairs, and without looking at Sam she said, "Sheriff Kinsley wants —"

"Quiet, Beth!" Kinsley rapped out.

Wallace looked briefly, without curiosity, at

Kinsley, his eyes chill and unfriendly.

Kinsley said to Wallace with a deceptive mildness, "Wait for what, Wallace?"

"I've got business with Miss Hilliard."

"Have you, now?" Kinsley said gently. "What is it?"

Wallace didn't even look at him. His glance dropped to the deed and then rose to Beth's face. "You selling Chevron?"

Beth looked at Sam, and there was only a careful watchfulness on his face. She knew he wanted Wallace to talk, wanted her to encourage him.

She said, "You know I am."

Wallace said quietly, "I'd like to buy it."

Of all things that this man could have said, Beth was least prepared for this. Here he was, a fugitive who had almost killed a man, appearing calmly in front of the sheriff and asking to buy Chevron. There was an air of unreality about it that held Beth motionless, almost stunned. She glanced at Sam again, for help this time, and saw the slow surprise in his face. Beth, knowing he would break this when he thought best, said weakly to Wallace, "I'm selling my two-thirds share of Chevron to Mr. Gove."

"For how much?"

"That's no business of yours!" Beth flared.

"It's yours," Wallace drawled, "because I'll

151

give you more than Gove will." His big hand moved forward and put a canvas sack on the desk now. When it left his fingers she heard the solid chunk of coins, many of them. "Two hundred and fifty double eagles," Wallace murmured. "There's as much more as you name."

Beth didn't move, watching Sam. She saw him shift his glance from Wallace to Gove, amazed questioning in his eyes. He looked at the coins again, and then Wallace went on, "Ten thousand. Fifteen thousand. Just name it, Miss Hilliard."

All of them were silent now. Nothing in Sam's expression gave a clue to what she should do, and Beth turned to Gove. She surprised a hard, steady alertness in his eyes that were watching Wallace.

"You can't pass that up, Beth," Gove said quietly to her.

Sam said flatly, "Wait a minute," and stepped closer to Wallace.

"Would you buy Chevron, pay that money, if you knew you were going to jail tomorrow? Maybe for life?"

A faint frown creased Wallace's forehead. His attention narrowed, and he looked silently at Beth, then at Gove, and then at Kinsley.

"Yes."

Sam's gun came up with an effortless ease, and it was cocked, pointing at

152

Wallace's midriff.

"Then go on with your business," Sam said heavily, "because you're going to jail afterward."

Beth always remembered later the kind of disdainful expression with which Wallace regarded Sam's gun, and then the slow lift of his glance as he looked at Sam.

"What have you dreamed up now, Sheriff?"

Sam said flatly, "Seegrist is upstairs with his chest caved in. When you shot his horse out from under him yesterday it fell on him."

Wallace shook his head slowly. "I didn't shoot his horse."

And then from behind Beth came Tom Hyam's quiet, almost sinister voice.

"You're the man who pulled off into the brush a mile below that second ford yesterday afternoon when I came in sight."

Gove wheeled sharply and stared at Hyam.

Sam didn't take his eyes off Wallace, only said, "Come here, Hyam."

Hyam came over, accepting the cold wicked stare of Wallace without seeming to notice it.

Sam said to Hyam, "You saw him near the second ford yesterday afternoon?"

"I did."

"Why didn't you tell me?"

Hyam drawled with a faint contempt. "I didn't put the two together till I saw the horse. And I didn't recognize this man, never having

153

seen him before. Would it have done you any good, Sheriff, if I'd told you I saw a man at the second ford, yet couldn't describe him accurately or tell you who he was?" He added dryly, "You were sure enough, anyway, I gathered."

Sam stepped up and lifted Wallace's gun from its holster. He said, "That's all I want. You'll sit in jail, Wallace, until Seegrist is recovered, and then you'll stand trial for attempted murder. If he dies it'll be just plain murder."

Beth watched Wallace's face and saw no trace of dismay, only a cold, hard contempt. He even smiled faintly, recklessly, at Kinsley, and then his gaze shuttled to Hyam. "Remarkable eyesight," he murmured and then his glance settled on Beth. She saw again in his eyes that old dislike of her. He said dryly, "My offer is good until your friends hang me, Miss Hilliard."

It was over then; Sam, gun still in hand, followed Wallace out onto the porch. Her dun, Beth saw, was tied at the rack beside Kinsley's horse. Beth followed Kinsley out onto the veranda, and as she watched Wallace tramp proudly down the steps a sudden and inexplicable doubt assailed her.

When Beth was gone and they were alone Gove regarded Hyam with an expressionless face.

Hyam said quietly, "I think you better cut me in, Gove."

For half a minute they looked at each other, and then Gove said gently, "Why do you?"

"I saw Chance in the brush."

Gove's face altered a little, only faintly, shrewdly, and then he nodded his head ever so slightly.

"All right," he said.

CHAPTER 9

Dave was roused in late morning by somebody tugging at his leg. He came awake in his bunk to see an elderly man, whose malarial-yellow face was bisected by a mournful roan mustache, regarding him through the cell bars.

It was stifling hot in here, and when Dave swung his feet down to the floor he felt the cool spot where he had sweat through his shirt back. He shook his head to clear it and then looked about him with a drugged disinterest. Vermillion County's jail was a two-cell affair built of the cliff's red sandstone; the bars were four-by-four timbers ironed on two sides with old wagon tires to discourage sawing. Dave had the cell next to the sheriff's office, through which he had entered last night. There was a door at the other end of the cell block and a timber- and heavy screen-barred window in the wall opposite.

"Want to wash?" the jailer asked.

Dave nodded, and the old man went down and unlocked the rear door. Returning, he

156

removed the heavy padlock from Dave's cell door and stepped aside, bringing up his worn carbine to the slack of his arm with a professional ease.

Dave rose and went out the rear door and shut his eyes against the blazing noonday sun. When he opened them again he looked around him. The sheriff's office and jail were placed to one side of a littered strip of ground surrounded by a high board fence. Access to it, save by a locked gate, was through an old false-front store building on a side street that served as the Vermillion County courthouse. The other end of the yard abutted the steep sandstone cliff, under which was a weathered horse shed.

Water was piped to a trough beside it from the feed-stable well, which was only a hundred feet away across the back lots.

Dave went over to the trough, which had overflowed into a tramped pool of mud, and soaked his head in the water. He glanced back once toward the jail and saw his jailer standing in the shadow of the door, one shoulder propped against the jamb, rifle slacked from his hand.

The water wakened him, and he ran his neckerchief over his dripping black hair and retied it around his neck, then tramped back to the guard.

157

"Your grub's come," the guard said.

He stepped aside, carefully keeping out of Dave's reach, then dropped in behind him and locked him in his cell with a tray of food. The stifling heat of the cell block took away Dave's appetite.

He ate little and drank his coffee, and then settled back in the bunk and rolled himself a smoke and took stock of his situation. It couldn't, he conceded, be much worse. The sole consolation to be salvaged from the whole mess was that he thought he'd stopped the sale of Chevron to Gove. He didn't give a damn about that, except that by interfering he'd been able to pay Ives back for the talk with Martha Macy.

The depth of his disgust with himself and with all of them put a lethargy upon him that he didn't even fight. He was in the hands of Kinsley, who, if he chose, could make his offense bailable. But neither Ives nor Buckley, his sole friends here, could come out in the open with bail for him. Which made his freedom improbable.

His jailer came back then and unlocked the door and said, "Go up front. The sheriff wants to see you."

Dave threw his cigarette away and stepped out into the sheriff's office. Kinsley, despite the heat, had not shed his coat, and Dave knew it was for the sake of the dignity of his office. He sat at a rickety desk, over which was a gun-rack holding a half-dozen shotguns and rifles. The four walls of the small room were papered almost solidly with yellowed reward dodgers.

"Sit down," Kinsley said quietly. "Wait till I finish this. Old Decker treating you all right?"

Dave said he was. He sank into a chair and waited the minute until Kinsley finished his writing and tilted back in his swivel chair. Kinsley laced the fingers of his two hands together across the small of his neck said idly, "Those cells are pretty miserable."

Dave didn't answer, and Kinsley regarded him speculatively. "You know, you don't have to put up with this, Wallace."

Dave said dryly, "You put up with anything a sheriff tells you to."

"Not if you'll straighten this out."

"What do you want to know?"

"I want you to admit you shot Seegrist's horse."

"But I didn't."

Kinsley's fingers unlaced, and he swung his chair back level and said earnestly, "But, man, you've worked Seegrist over twice, and you threatened in public to run him out of the country. That's prime evidence."

"I will run him out too," Dave said quietly.

Kinsley looked solemn. "But why?"

"You know why. I told you the first night. I don't change that story."

Kinsley looked at him thoughtfully and said, "Let's hear it again."

"I met Seegrist over in the Mesquite Hills. A bunch of Chevron horses were grazing in the brush around his camp. I stopped and had a smoke with him and mentioned Tip Macy. I knew Tip in Montana, and I'd read he'd died in a blizzard. I didn't believe it and I asked Seegrist about it."

"You mean you put it up to him that way?"

"No. We kind of danced around it," Dave said slowly. "He wasn't putting out anything about Macy, and I was asking a lot of questions. When I saw it was no good I asked him about water on the desert. He told me about a short cut to what he called the Bunchgrass Tanks. Said he'd come across two days before and there was plenty of water. I thanked him and lined out with my pack horse. The Tanks were dry, and he knew it."

Before Dave finished speaking Kinsley was shaking his head slowly. "Wallace, it wasn't Seegrist. You say those horses were branded Chevron?"

Dave nodded.

Kinsley said dryly, "How'd they get across the desert to the Mesquite Hills?"

"I don't know."

"The answer to that," Kinsley observed flatly, "is that they didn't. There's water in just two places on that desert, and both those places are stage stations, run by McAuliffe and Kearney. Anything that crosses that desert, man or beast, has to hit those two spots. And neither Seegrist nor a bunch of horses stopped at either place, because I checked."

Dave didn't answer.

"So that," Kinsley remarked idly, "makes you out a liar."

Dave only shook his head. "You're a careful man, Kinsley," he began. "You like to check. I'll give you some more to check, so you can make a bigger liar out of me."

Kinsley looked puzzled, skeptical.

"I came into this country to find out how Tip Macy died. You say he died in a blizzard. I found out different. He was shot in the back at Chevron's boundary-line camp. You didn't know that, did you?"

Kinsley's pause was a half minute long. "I don't know it now," he said derisively.

"Then check it," Dave drawled. "Check it with Gove, because he told me. Check it with Miss Hilliard, because he told her. And check it with Martha Macy, because Gove told her too."

He stood up then, and Kinsley sat there, a faint doubt in his eyes, watching him.

161

"I'll do that," he promised quietly.

Decker appeared in the doorway then, and Dave headed for the door to the cell block. He paused then and turned and said, "When you've checked that you might check Hyam too."

"I'll do that too," Kinsley said.

As Dave turned he thought he detected a faint note of amusement in Kinsley's stubborn face.

Back in his cell he lay down again. It was too hot to smoke, and he stared stupidly at the ceiling. He didn't expect anything to come from his revelation to Kinsley about Tip Macy's death, but he might have succeeded in planting a single doubt in Kinsley's thick head. Mention of Hyam, of course, was simple prodding. He knew that men like Hyam couldn't be traced or questioned, for they spent a lifetime covering their tracks for men like Kinsley.

He turned on his side and hoped bitterly that Ives would be satisfied now. The single clue to Tip Macy's murder, gleaned in his talk with Martha Macy, he had neglected in order to help Ives help Beth Hilliard. And that clue would now wait days or weeks or months, and maybe forever, to be tracked down. Seco camp had waited on Ives.

Presently, in disgust, he slept.

When he wakened, again drugged with the

162

still heat, he saw Decker standing beside Beth Hilliard outside the bars.

Decker said, "I'll have to lock you in, Miss Hilliard. Sheriff's orders."

"All right."

Dave came to his feet, and Beth Hilliard stepped into the cell. He motioned awkwardly toward the bunk, and she sat down on it. Already her upper lip was beaded with perspiration, but her fresh dress looked crisp and neat.

She was embarrassed, now that they were alone, and Dave didn't help her out. He hunkered down against the opposite wall and regarded her almost with hostility. From the day he had climbed into the Vermillion stage until this meeting they had not exchanged a friendly word. In whatever direction his search for Tip Macy's killer took him it had crossed this girl's path sooner or later. As the condition of Ives's help, Dave had been thrown with her again — until now, he regarded her as his own private cross to bear. He wished fervently that she was ugly and unattractive, so that her blind loyalty to Gove and the flaming stupidity with which she defended him could be considered the natural act of an unloved woman. Instead, she was proud and womanly and beloved, a person to be circumvented and handled with a kindly tactfulness. And he was finding out he wasn't much good at either.

"I felt I had to see you again," she said now. "I – I came on business."

Dave nodded. "How's Seegrist?"

"Better today." She was watching him closely as she talked, and Dave knew she was trying to see him in the new light of Chevron's buyer. There was a kind of truce declared in her hazel eyes – as if, now that he might buy Chevron, he should be treated as a business equal instead of a criminal gunman. It fanned some deep obstinacy within him, and it must have shown in his eyes, for Beth smiled and said hastily, "About buying the Chevron."

Dave inclined his head.

"I've talked it over with Jess. We both agree I can't afford not to take it. That is" – she spoke hesitantly – "if you're serious."

"Serious?" A quick resentment mounted in him and he asked dryly, "Were those double eagles made of wood?"

He saw the temper rise in her eyes, but she had control over herself. "I didn't mean that. But you mentioned more money. You said ten or fifteen thousand."

He nodded.

"But that's just like saying two million or three million dollars," she pointed out, reproof and a little condescension in her voice. "One is a third more than the other. It's – well, too

164

vague. I didn't know if you meant it."

"I did."

"So your offer is what?"

Dave rubbed his chin thoughtfully, a kind of cross-grained humor upon him. He was being patronized and his instinct was to retaliate.

He murmured soberly, "Well, I guess you'd rather have the five thousand. Let's make it fifteen."

A small despair was in her eyes. She stamped her foot and said in exasperation, "There! How can I believe you're serious? You add a third onto your offer in a second, just as if you were dealing in stage money!"

Dave said soberly, "All right. We'll make it ten if fifteen doesn't suit you."

Beth rose from the cell bunk, and Dave saw she was coldly furious. "All right, Mr. Wallace, we'll make it ten, since you can't talk sensibly. And I doubt if you have ten or fifteen thousand or if you even intend to buy Chevron!"

"A week will tell," Dave drawled.

"I'll wait a week then. And now I'd like to get out of here."

Dave walked over to the bars and called, "Decker," and waited.

He and Beth looked at each other. Beth was angry, and Dave, seeing it now, was faintly ashamed of his rawhiding.

Beth said suddenly, "There's something else

165

I wanted to tell you too. I don't want to now, but I wanted to before I came, so I suppose I'll tell you." She hesitated before she said, almost defiantly, "I don't believe you shot at Ed Seegrist."

Dave just stared at her, mute with amazement. Decker came in then, and before he could unlock the door Dave said, "Why don't you?"

"Call it a woman's instinct," Beth said tartly. "I just don't believe you would. Good day."

She went out, and Dave put both hands on the timbers and watched her go. Afterward he turned back to his bunk and sat down, and he was smiling. He thought he understood now why Ives wanted to help Beth Hilliard. There was something so feminine and honest in the way she'd said this that Dave felt a contrary and unaccountable liking for her. He'd baited her, half in contempt, and she'd risen to his bait. But there was something so clearheaded and forthright about her that she'd ignored it and spoken the truth, though it favored him.

He was sitting there minutes later, pondering it, when the office door opened and Sheriff Kinsley came in and tramped up to the bars.

"You know," Kinsley said, his voice at once angry and sardonic, "you're really a cabinet-piece liar, Wallace. Beth says Gove has never mentioned Tip Macy to her. Or to you, that she knows of."

He added with quiet malice as he turned away, "I hope you have a long and pleasant stay here."

He went out, and Dave sat there. He marveled quietly at this woman. She would tell him honestly that she did not believe him guilty of attempted murder, for which he was jailed, and in the next moment she would lie blandly to a sheriff who might hold him in jail for months as a result of her lie. He decided then that whatever she was, she wasn't the fool he'd thought her.

The afternoon waned and his supper came, and then darkness, and still the heat didn't lift. By the aid of the lamp in the wall bracket in the corridor he tried to read a paper Decker had given him. The perspiration from his forehead ran down in his eyes until he gave up and lay down on his bunk.

When Decker came to blow the lamp out he didn't even speak or move. He let the ribbon of his memory go back over all this, and he could see no way out.

The sounds of the night carousing at the saloons came to him, and he had a wild and ungovernable impulse to smash this cell even if they killed him for it.

And then it went, and he put his mind to all its cunning, and at the end of an hour he knew it was useless. He was here to stay as long as Kinsley's whim dictated.

He was lying there, coaxing a drugged, hot sleep when he heard the slow, quiet whine of metal giving under pressure. Listening, he heard it again and silently sat up.

A heavy thump sounded on the plank floor outside his cell door, and he thought he heard a movement outside the window.

Kneeling, he struck a match and poked it through the bars, and the orange light from it picked up the sheen of metal. He reached out and put his hand on a gun.

Drawing it toward him, his first thought was of Ives and his second of trickery.

Striking another match, he looked at the gun, a worn Colt .44, and saw the lead tips of the cartridges showing in the cylinder.

And then he saw the piece of paper rolled up and thrust inside the barrel, barely showing white at the gun's muzzle.

He pulled it out and unrolled it and read the bold writing:

SEEGRIST IS DEAD.

The match died, and kneeling there in the dark, he supplied what the writer of the note had left unwritten.

With Seegrist dead, he was in here for keeps.

168

But not with this gun, he thought.

Sitting on his bunk in the darkness now, he knew it was Ives who'd got the gun to him. And furthermore, he'd probably beat the news of Seegrist's death down from Hilliard.

Dave weighed the various methods of escape open to him now, savoring with a slow pleasure. He could call Decker in now and hold the gun on him and make Decker free him. But, remembering the taciturn capability of Decker, Dave knew that wouldn't work. He'd refuse to unlock the door.

He sat there for an hour, thinking, and finally he had his plan worked out.

He did not trust himself to sleep during the two-hour wait until dawn, and he was wide awake when he heard the town come to life.

When Decker came in later the cell block was almost cool, and Dave was lying awake in his bunk.

Decker said amiably, "Cool enough to sleep?"

Dave said it was and came to a sitting position and stretched and stood up as Decker unlocked his cell and stepped aside, rifle held at his side.

As he had done the day before, Dave led the way out the rear door into the yard. His gun was in the waistband of his pants under his shirt, and he tramped leisurely over to the trough, where he washed.

Bent over now, he looked back at Decker. Habit, he knew, was strong in a man, and Decker yesterday had not stepped out into the yard but he remained in the doorway, watching his prisoner. If he did the same this morning Dave was safe.

Decker looked over the yard, its early-morning coolness inviting, but he stayed in the doorway. Dave finished washing and started back to the cell-block door, looking around him with a curiosity that Decker wouldn't find strange.

And then, as he had done the day before, Decker stepped inside the cell block toward the inside corner to allow Dave to enter and still not be close to him. There was a precious second there when Decker could not see him.

And in that second Dave, not missing step, lifted out his gun and held it against his leg.

He walked through the door, took a step into the room, and Decker started to fall in behind him, rifle held at his side.

Dave wheeled swiftly then, lifting the gun hip-high, and with his free hand slapping down the barrel of Decker's carbine.

It was done so swiftly that Decker found himself face to face with Dave, his own gun at his side and Dave's gun pointing at his belly.

Dave said, "That's about it."

Under his dolorous mustaches Decker's

mouth was open with surprise.

Dave said, "Quiet, now."

He could see in Decker's eyes now that the old man was considering his chances and instantly rejecting them.

Decker said mildly, "All right, son. Just don't get nervous."

"Let go your rifle."

Decker did, and Dave let it fall to the floor. He backed away and motioned Decker into the cell.

What he did next was not to his liking, but there was no choice. When Decker stepped into the cell Dave rapped him smartly over the head with his gun barrel. Decker's knees buckled, and he folded quietly to the floor.

Dave got his Stetson, shut the door, locked it, closed the rear door, rammed his gun in his waistband, and stepped into the sheriff's office. It was empty.

He went on through into the yard and headed for the courthouse. When he was almost to it a boy carrying a tray of food from the restaurant stepped out of the door.

Dave grinned at him and said, "Take that back and I'll be over and eat it in a minute."

"You out?" the boy asked.

"That's it. And hungry."

The boy turned back, and Dave followed him into the building. The old store had been partitioned off into the county offices, leaving a corridor running through the building. Dave walked through this, parted with the boy on the street after he'd given him his order for breakfast, and then turned down-street, walking leisurely.

There were a few people on the streets, clerks opening stores and sweeping boardwalks, swampers cleaning out saloons. He gave a placid good morning to them all and turned in at the feed stable.

To the hostler, the one he had spoken to his first night in Vermillion, he said, "Remember me? I was brought in the other night by the sheriff."

"Sure. You was ridin' Beth Hilliard's buckskin."

"That's right. Saddle him up, will you?"

"Everythin' settled?" the hostler asked amiably.

"Right as rain," Dave replied calmly.

In five minutes, during which he watched the street with a careful eye for any sign of alarm, Beth Hilliard's horse was brought out to him.

He took the reins, said, "Kinsley said he'd settle with you," stepped into the saddle, and calmly rode out of town in the direction of Hilliard.

CHAPTER 10

Arnie Chance rode into Chevron around mid-afternoon. He turned his horse into the corral, but not the pasture, and tramped up to the bunkhouse. He paused at the door to look inside, waiting a moment for his eyes to get accustomed to the dimness of the room.

Pete Framm was sitting at the stump bench by the big table, patching a bridle.

"Gove left?" Chance asked.

"No."

Chance stepped out and went on up to the house and let himself into the office without knocking. Pausing just inside the door, he looked around the dark room, and his glance came to rest on Gove asleep on the worn sofa.

Quietly Chance stepped over to the sofa and looked down at Gove, his bleach eyes reflective and hard. The cut on his cheekbone, where Dave Wallace had kicked him, was healing, but the bruise was still livid, and it gave a tough cast to his long face. He looked at Gove a full minute, studying the features which were almost saintly in sleep. *He never lets go, not even when he's sleeping,* Chance thought, and a bitter smile of admiration moved his thin lips.

He took off his Stetson and put it on the desk and then went over and turned the key in the door which let onto the living room adjoining. He came back to Gove then and shook him by the shoulder and stood above him while he roused and swung his feet to the floor.

Arnie sat down then at the worn chair by the desk.

"You got it to him?" Gove asked.

Arnie nodded. "He read the note too."

Gove rose then. He walked to the window, his tall shoulders stooped, and stood there, back to Chance, looking out.

Arnie lifted his sack of tobacco from his shirt pocket and rolled a cigarette. His movements were mechanical, for he was watching Gove with a kind of alert speculation in his eyes.

He licked his cigarette and put it in his mouth with one motion, and then he drew a match from his shirt pocket and had his thumbnail on it, ready to strike it, when he asked a question.

"You see the hole in this thing, Jess?"

Gove turned to him, and his white eyebrows were pulled together in question. "Hole? There isn't any."

"What if Wallace doesn't drift?"

174

Gove said quietly, "If he's not drifting now he'll drift after what happens tonight."

"Don't be too sure. He's an Injun." Chance paused, and his hand started to his cheek. "I hope he don't," he said thinly, his bleach eyes cold and wicked with the memory of Wallace's kicking him in the face. "I'd admire to see him again."

"You won't," Gove said. He turned to face Chance, and his expression was one of musing. "You're forgetting Kinsley. He's stubborn. After what happens tonight he'll get Wallace if it takes him a lifetime. Wallace knows it."

Chance said, "Wallace is a better man."

"But not so good a man he can take on every fighting hand on this slope."

Chance nodded. "Maybe he will drift then."

Gove asked, "What gun did you give him?"

"My old .44."

"Then carry a .44 tonight," Gove said. He added soberly, "Be careful tonight, Arnie. Just be careful."

"Don't worry about it."

Gove went over to the worn sofa and sat down. "Now about Hyam. Send him to the mill road above town."

"He'll be spooky," Chance drawled.

"He's greedy," Gove observed. "Greedy men are always spooky. But they're always greedier than they are spooky."

Chance smiled then and rose. He had forgotten to light the cigarette that had been pasted in the corner of his mouth. Now he removed it and threw it on the floor and yawned. Gove rose too.

"Make it nine o'clock," Gove said. "I'll let Hyam see me around town first. Now go get some sleep."

Arnie nodded and went over to the door.

"Arnie," Gove said quietly.

Chance turned and Gove murmured, "Just play it careful. Remember, this will get us Chevron."

Chance nodded and went out, crossing toward the bunkhouse. It was deserted at this hour. A big blue-bottle fly circled and yawed and collided with the window and circled off again, droning around the room.

It was a sleepy sound, and when Chance sat down on his bunk and pulled off his boots and lay down he was sure he could sleep.

But he couldn't. He heard Gove tramp past toward the corral, and he lay there awhile, thinking of the old man. Oddly, he remembered the night two years after they'd buried Joe Hilliard. The night after the funeral Jess Gove, whom he, along with everybody else, believed was next thing to a saint, had called him in.

There'd never been another conversation like

that in the world, Chance thought. His memory of it was vivid, unforgettable, and would remain so until he died. Gove had been seated at the desk. Arnie stood before him, hat in hand.

"I've been watching you, Chance," Gove said in his mild summer-soft voice. "You're a thorough hard case." Gove had looked at him with a different look, a kind of cunning, sharp, boring look that seemed to peel away all the careful pretense Chance had so carefully built. He'd felt revealed to Gove as a tough, ruthless Texan who had known trouble and wasn't afraid of it. He hadn't answered.

Gove had said, "Forget Beth Hilliard, Chance. Forget the name of Hilliard. I'm Chevron now. I'll own it and I'll have power. You'll have money. Stick with me and you'll be rich. Don't and I'll see you buried. How does it sound?"

"It sounds like sense," Arnie had said.

Gove had nodded. "I thought it would. From now on you're Chevron's foreman."

That's all there was to it, and he'd stuck and he was on his way to being rich, and Gove was getting Chevron.

Somebody shouted something down at the barn, and Chance idly tried to identify the voice. Then the fly started again, and he listened to it with half an ear, thinking now of tonight.

It wouldn't be hard. Just one bad second and that was all.

Now he heard the house door shut and he listened for somebody to pass, and nobody did. Lying there, he thought who it might be, speculating, and he couldn't guess. And because he had nothing else to think of, the speculation annoyed him. It grew into an obsession, until he finally rose in restlessness and walked in his sock feet to the window.

Martha Macy was standing out in front of the house, looking up the valley. Then head down, she started to stroll out into the meadow, her path aimless, her pace slow.

Idly curious now, Chance watched her as she strolled over to the big windfall at the edge of the timber and sat on it. She was out for a look at the evening, and Chance remained there at the window, staring at her simply because he was both restless and half hypnotized with drowsiness.

And then he saw her turn and look into the timber. It was a brief, casual thing; only it stuck in Chance's mind that she seemed as if she were looking for someone.

His interest sharpened now, and he watched her closely. But she seemed only to be sitting there, looking at the valley. Presently she rose, smoothed her skirt, and started back for the house, walking slowly.

But the thought persisted in Chance's mind, and he watched her intently until she disappeared in the house. Then his glance shuttled to the windfall by the meadow. The very fact that after she'd turned her head he had seen her do nothing else suspicious only made him more certain he was right. Granted there was someone in the timber, who was it? Not Wallace, because Wallace was in jail.

But he wasn't!

Chance straightened up, instantly alert. Then he rejected the thought. How could Wallace have known he was breaking out today? But now the suspicion was there, and Chance's mind must be satisfied.

He pulled on his boots and left the bunkhouse and tramped out the fifty yards to the windfall. He hurried a little because dusk was settling.

Skirting the windfall, he stopped at the edge of the timber and looked around suspiciously. There was nothing to see, nobody here, no sign anybody had been here. But the lack of something tangible only fed his suspicions. He searched at the base of individual trees now and finally arrived at a big jack pine whose trunk was large enough to hide a man.

He knelt and studied the deep humus of rotted needles there and saw plainly enough an indentation. Fingering away some of the needles, he saw the marks of boot heels in the soft humus. His speculation narrowed now. Somebody had been here since the tracks with the boot heels had been made.

Patiently he searched for other tracks and found one — the track of a moccasin. A little farther out, where sparse grass was growing, he found the track again. And the grass which had been bent down was still rising.

Chance slowly came to his feet, adding all this up with a patient viciousness. Mrs. Macy had been talking to two men at different times. The second man wore moccasins, the first half boots. There was only one person she had been warned against talking to, and that was Dave Wallace. And since she had talked to a man secretly it was safe to assume that one of these men, the one with half boots, was Wallace. The one in the moccasins he didn't care about.

A slow, cold rage was in Chance now as he looked back at the house. He needed proof and he knew that he would never get it from Martha Macy by force. Gove wouldn't stand for it, because Martha Macy was Beth Hilliard's friend. There was another way. He went back to the house and knocked once on the living-room door and stepped inside.

Martha Macy was just lighting the overhead lamp above the living-room table, and when she saw Chance she paused, her arms still lifted to raise the lamp.

Chance drawled amiably, "I just come to tell you you don't have to hide it any more. Ask him in next time."

"Hide what?" Martha asked blankly.

Chance nodded toward the timber. "I saw the tracks."

Martha's face altered imperceptibly, and Chance, seeing it, was merciless. He said musingly, "Maybe Wallace was right, and we been on the wrong track."

"What are you talking about?" Martha asked carefully. She lowered her arms slowly, intent now on Chance.

"Maybe Tip wasn't stealin' cattle," Chance said idly. "Kinsley don't think so."

"He doesn't?" Martha asked swiftly.

"Not after what Wallace told him."

"What did he tell him?"

"Just what you told Wallace," Chance drawled.

"You mean, Wallace —" Martha stopped, some inner caution warning her. But it was too late. She saw Chance's bleach eyes come wholly alert, lose their amiability. She'd been tricked.

"So you saw him," Chance drawled.

"I don't know what you're talking about."

Chance came slowly around the table now and faced her.

"When was this?" he asked thinly.

Martha said coldly, "Careful, Arnie. It's none of your business what I do or ever have done."

"What did you tell him?"

Martha didn't answer.

Chance reached out and grabbed her by the wrist and twisted her arm around behind her back. She couldn't fight against the quiet strength of him, and when he bent her arm back she cried in pain.

"What did you tell him?" Chance repeated.

The door came open then, and Pete Framm stepped into the room. Chance looked up at the sound of the door opening, and he was utterly motionless as Pete came slowly up to the table.

Pete Framm said quietly, ominously, murderously, "Get away from her, Chance."

Arnie Chance let go her arm. His face was bland, almost amused, and he stepped away from her, not even looking at her.

Chance said idly, "Next time you bust in on a man and wife you better knock."

Pete Framm's face had been tense with wildness. But now the shock of what he had heard washed out the anger, and he turned amazed eyes on Martha.

It was for that moment Chance had been waiting. He raised a leg and kicked savagely at the table. Sliding, it caught Pete Framm across the hips and jackknifed him across it, and then he fell, clawing awkwardly for his gun.

Chance dived at him and landed square on his chest with both knees. It drove the wind from Pete's lungs with a great soughing groan, and then Chance slashed down at his unprotected chin with a swift, savage hook. Pete's head turned under the blow, and, Chance hooked in another blow with his left hand, catching Pete flush on the shelf of the jaw.

Then carefully he came off Pete Framm, who did not move a muscle.

Chance looked wickedly at Martha and said, "When he wakes up tell him he's through here."

He went silently out the door, heading swiftly for the corral.

Martha, her terror draining away now, came over and knelt by Pete Framm. She shook him by the shoulders and tried to rouse him and could not. In panic she thought he might be dead, and then she calmed herself long enough to think of water. She ran to the kitchen and came back with a basin of water and doused it on Pete's face.

Slowly, taking minutes, it seemed, he opened his eyes. She was kneeling beside him now, watching him.

When he tried to sit up she helped him. He sat there a moment, his eyes dull, shaking his head from side to side. He essayed to stand now, and again Martha helped him, guiding his hand to the edge of the overturned table to brace him.

Erect, Pete drew three deep breaths, shook his head sharply, and then his eyes came into focus.

He looked searchingly at Martha and said slowly, "Was that right? What he said?"

"It was a rotten lie to trick you!" Martha said vehemently.

Pete wheeled and lunged for the door and had it halfway open when Martha said, "He's gone. It's no use, Pete."

Pete stopped, then closed the door slowly, and looked over at her.

"God, what a sucker I am," he said bitterly.

There was a pitying sympathy in Martha's face, and Pete came over to her. "Did he hurt you?"

"No, no," she said quickly. She was watching him with wide, luminous eyes, as if slowly something was being revealed to her.

"Why did you do that, Pete?" she asked in a low voice.

"I been kinda lookin' out for you," Pete said soberly. "You figured I would after what I said to you that night in the hotel kitchen, didn't you?"

Martha's glance fell, and she did not answer him, only said, "He told me you were through here, Pete."

184

"So are you," Pete said flatly. "I don't aim to leave you where he can reach you."

Martha looked up at him, and the corners of her eyes were wet.

Seeing it, Pete asked awkwardly, "What's the matter?"

"I don't know." She turned away. "I guess — it's just — well, I'm not used to hearing anything like that."

"You're goin' to hear plenty more of it from me," Pete said quietly. "Now tell me where I can take you that he can't reach you," and he added, almost shyly, "Martha."

Chance tied his horse at the tie rail in front of the hotel and looked speculatively at the lamplit Olympus. Had the word about Wallace's break reached town yet? It didn't matter; only he would like to know.

Deliberately he tramped up the hotel steps and went into the lobby.

Hyam was behind the corner desk, a newspaper spread out on the counter before him, reading.

When he looked up and saw Chance he closed the newspaper and quietly laid it aside and said, "Evening," his voice questioning, faintly sardonic.

Chance nodded and put his elbows on the desk and regarded Hyam with a kind of amiable indifference. "The boss wants to see

185

you," he murmured.

"Bring him in."

Chance shook his head. "Won't do."

"I'm to go to him, eh?" Hyam asked dryly. "I'll bet he's outside of town, waiting for me in the dark."

"A right guess."

"With a gun."

Chance smiled. "That's a chance a man takes when he sticks his nose into a stranger's business." He added dryly, "Carry a gun yourself if it'll make you feel better."

"I will, my friend," Hyam murmured. "It'll make me feel better, too. Where do I meet him?"

"Where the sawmill road forks off."

Chance nodded and turned away from the desk, and Hyam said then, "Some news just came up from Vermillion that might interest you."

Chance paused and looked at him questioningly.

"Wallace broke out of jail this morning," Hyam said.

Chance frowned and was quiet a moment and then said, "It ought to interest you some, too."

"It does," Hyam admitted. "He'll come to see me sooner or later. Point is, he might have money with him to change my story of who I saw by the second ford. And that story, as Gove

186

damn well knows, is for sale." He held out his palm and tapped it with his finger. "Don't forget this. It itches almost all the time."

"Tell Gove," Chance said and went out.

He crossed the street and halfway across it looked back at the hotel. He saw Hyam moving around in the lobby. Now he looked up and down the street, which he saw was empty, and then stepped quietly into the deep shadow made by the old warehouse next to the Olympus.

He waited there until he saw Hyam leave the hotel, heading downstreet for the feed stable. And still he waited, not smoking, keeping an eye on the street. In a few minutes Hyam rode by him, crossed the timber bridge, and headed up the sloping wagon road.

Chance gave him a few minutes and then crossed the street swiftly toward the hotel, peering up- and down-street as he moved.

Untying the reins of his horse, he led him down to the edge of the stream and into it and tied him to one of the bridge timbers.

Now he came back to the hotel steps. He paused in their shadow until a man crossed from Rollins' store to the Olympus. Then swiftly he mounted the steps and tiptoed into the lobby and listened.

Somebody out in the kitchen was making a racket with the pans, but that was all he could hear.

Heading straight for the stairs, he climbed them noiselessly and paused at the head of the stair well. Down the corridor a lamp in a wall bracket was burning dimly, its wick turned down.

Beyond it was the window, and it was for this Chance headed. Coiled up on the floor by the window was a length of knotted rope fastened to a heavy long-shanked hook bolted into the window frame. This was the hotel's fire escape. He moved the loop of the rope over the hook once or twice, making certain it worked freely.

Then, moving over, he softly hoisted the window. The chatter of the Little Dun, below him and only a few yards off, drifted up to him.

Now he turned back down the hall and at Ed Seegrist's door he paused and listened again. He listened for a noise downstairs or within the room, and he could hear neither.

He reached for the doorknob now and paused, as if musing. Then slowly his right hand went to his holster and lifted his gun and cocked it noiselessly.

Now he turned the doorknob gently, gently opened the door.

Ed Seegrist was sleeping, his lamp turned low.

Chance opened the door wide, raised his gun, took careful sight, and fired. The shot bellowed in the stillness.

Afterward he closed the door gently, moved noiselessly to the corridor window, threw the rope out, put a leg over the sill, and slid down it. He could hear someone running through the lobby below.

Once on the ground, he gave the rope plenty cf slack, then flipped it smartly. Nothing happened. He did it again, and this time the rope came off its hook, slithering over the sill above, and fell to the ground. Whoever was climbing the stairs now wouldn't see it.

He let it lie there and stepped down the bank into the stream. Now he was below the level of the ground on which the hotel was standing, and he waded the stream down to his horse tied to the bridge.

While he was climbing into the saddle under the bridge a man started to yell from the hotel porch.

Chance paid him no attention. He rode on under the bridge, keeping to the stream, and was presently in the dark shadows in the rear of the store buildings.

He rode leisurely past them, the clatter of the stream hiding the sound of his horse's wading.

When he was through town he put his horse up the bank, climbed the grade, and was lost in the darkness of the night.

CHAPTER 11

The yelling of the cook from the porch of the hotel brought a couple of men to the door of the Olympus. When they heard his message that a man was shot they shouted the news back into the barroom, and it emptied immediately.

Con Buckley gave his bartender instructions to stay on the job and then waddled out into the night. There was no use hurrying; he could carry this mountain of flesh only so fast, he thought wryly. Halfway across the road he looked at Rollins' store and stopped cold. On the steps was old Ives, a gunny sack of groceries over his shoulder, peering down street.

Con called to him, and Ives put the sack down and came out into the street.

"When did you get in?" Con asked.

"Ten minutes ago. I was comin' over."

"Wallace broke out this morning."

Ives just stared at him, disbelief in his face. Then he said, "That what all the racket's about?"

"Somebody's shot over at the hotel."

Ives fell in with him, and they went over to the hotel. Upstairs there was the tramping of many feet, and Con labored savagely to make the stairs. A dozen men were crowded into one room, and Con shoved his way through to the inside of the circle.

He saw Seegrist lying in bed, the fear finally gone from his face. His chest was wet with blood, which had flowed down onto the covers and soaked them.

He heard Ives breathing slowly beside him.

"Shot in his sleep," a man said grimly.

"Where's Hyam?"

A third man said bitterly, "Why look for Hyam? Wallace got to Seegrist, all right."

These men looked at each other and nodded, their faces grim and hard with disgust.

"Somebody better ride for Kinsley," one of them said.

"He's on his way already with Miss Hilliard."

Con, a look of distaste turning up the corners of his small mouth, turned away from the sight and waddled down the stairs. Behind him he could hear the murmur of discussion mounting, and it was all about the same thing. They were organizing a posse to hunt for Wallace and were debating whether or not to wait for Kinsley.

Out on the porch Con paused for breath. A

191

pair of punchers, saner than the others, were talking in low tones at the side of the hotel below the window, discussing the killer's escape. From upstairs a man was calling to them, and they were answering.

Ives was suddenly at his side. Con sighed and went down the steps, and Ives fell in beside him.

Con said presently in a bitter, cynical voice, "That's the neatest frame-up I ever saw carpentered."

Ives shook his head. "We'll see how tough he is now."

"Nobody's that tough." Con paused. "Who did it, Ives?"

Ives said sourly, "Gove's the only man who wants Wallace out of the country. I can't think of a better way to run him out."

Con looked sharply at him. "If he's run out, then Gove gets Chevron."

"It won't work," Ives said flatly. He left Con without another word and crossed to Rollins' store and picked up his gunny sack of groceries.

As he straightened up he was aware that there was a man standing beyond the light that came out of the door, watching him.

Ives peered at him, and the man stepped forward. He was a young puncher with a face that Ives couldn't place.

He came closer and said to Ives in a low

voice, "Wallace said to see you when I quit Chevron. I've quit."

"You're Pete Framm."

Pete nodded.

Ives said, "Let me get out of town first. I'll pick you up on the south road."

"I'm not alone."

Ives looked at him suspiciously, and Pete said, "Mrs. Macy's with me. Chance got it out of her tonight that she talked with Wallace. She can't stay at Chevron."

Ives said quickly, "Does he know she talked with me?"

"No."

"Bring her along," Ives said. "Let me go first."

Ives swung the sack of grub over his shoulder and tramped down to his horse. He swore bitterly to himself as he stepped into the saddle and pulled his mare around. Gove was warned now. If he knew Wallace had talked with Martha Macy he would reason that she had told Wallace about Macy's intention to go to the Seco camp instead of the boundary. Gove would know exactly how much Wallace knew of Tip Macy's strange death, and he would do whatever was necessary to cover his trail. Ives felt badly about that. Not because he cared about Macy, but because he'd promised Dave Wallace that he'd find Macy's killer in exchange for Dave's help. Dave had kept his part of the bargain; he'd helped Ives with Beth Hilliard, had even gone to jail to do it, and now faced a charge of murder because of that help. Just how tough and patient was Wallace? The big man didn't give a damn about Beth, and yet he was on the dodge now because he'd helped her. Ives didn't fool himself; Wallace would probably tell him he was through, and Ives, in bitter honesty, couldn't blame him.

A half mile beyond the grade into Hilliard he pulled off the road and dismounted in the darkness. A lot of things had to be done tonight and tomorrow, because this country would be combed by posses. He'd have to move fast and quick and find some way to reach Dave.

Presently he heard the two horses approaching and swung into the saddle and called, "Here."

When they approached Ives said, "We'll talk later," and pulled his horse off into the timber.

He was still camped at the same spot, the one Dave Wallace had picked in the dark and Ives had never bothered to change. Approaching it, he was casting back in his memory for the safest place he could think of for a camp, when he looked up and saw through the trees the flickering light from a fire.

When he rode up to the edge of the timber and reined up he saw Dave Wallace standing on the other side of the fire, out of the light, his gun held loosely in his hand.

When Dave saw the three horses and their riders he stepped back into the firelight, holstering his gun. His glance was quizzical as he looked from Ives to Martha Macy and then to Pete.

Pete said blankly, "I thought you were in jail."

"Was," Dave corrected. "Ives slipped me a gun."

He looked at the old wolfer.

Ives had one foot out of the stirrup and was leaning forward to dismount. Now he stopped and stared at Dave and said, "I never slipped you a gun."

They regarded each other a long moment, and then Ives said, "Ah," softly, bitterly. He slipped to the ground and faced Dave and said in a wry voice, "A half-hour ago in Hilliard, Seegrist was shot."

"A half-hour ago?" Dave echoed. "But the note that was rammed in the barrel of the gun said he'd died. That was after midnight last night."

"Sure," Ives said softly and waited for Dave to get the full significance of his news. Dave was looking at him, and now his face changed, registering a slow unbelief and then a hard and bitter acceptance.

Pete Framm and Martha Macy, still mounted, were watching Dave, and when he said nothing they looked at Ives.

"They knew he'd break out," Ives explained morosely. "They give him just time to make the ride from Vermillion to Hilliard and then killed Seegrist. They're gettin' up a posse now to hunt him."

Pete stepped out of the saddle and helped Martha to dismount. All of them gathered around the fire then, and Pete told of what happened at Chevron. It was the full sum of the bad news, and when Pete was finished he watched Dave and Ives. Dave, however, did not speak, and then Martha questioned Ives. The whole of what had happened thus far was explained to her, and when Ives was done Martha Macy was silent with wonder of it.

At last she said, "Ives, what is it Gove wants?"

"Chevron. For no money at all."

"And killing Tip is part of his getting it?"

Ives said gloomily, "I think it is." He looked at Dave, who was staring soberly at the fire, lost in thought. Ives said bitterly, reflectively, "Wallace, come into this country curious about Tip. I was curious about Gove. And because I could go into Chevron without bein' stopped, and Dave could bid for Chevron without bein' suspected, we made a trade." He grimaced.

196

"Well, we been licked. Dave is outlawed and Gove will get Chevron."

"No," Dave put in quietly.

Ives said sourly, "You think Beth will sell Chevron to you, now you're bein' hunted for Seegrist's killin'?"

"I know she will."

Ives regarded him with a tough skepticism. "I'll ask her."

"You won't do that, either," Dave said flatly. "That's my part of the bargain."

Ives said sourly, "You're just goin' into Hilliard, past Gove, past Chance, past Kinsley, past that mob of man hunters, and ask her?"

"That's right."

The quiet way he said it held Ives mute for a moment. A little while ago he had been scheming how to hold Dave to his bargain. And now he had a strange reluctance to do it. And feeling so, he came to a swift decision. "No. I don't hold any man to that bargain, Dave. It's wore out. You're on the dodge because you stuck to it, and I've done all I could about Macy. We'll call it quits."

Dave picked up a stick and poked the fire slowly. "Ives," he said slowly, "I hate a licking." He glanced up at the old wolfer, ignoring Martha and Pete. "I hate it so bad I won't take it. But that isn't it. I like Beth Hilliard."

Ives's unshaven jaw sagged in amazement.

"But you told me you had her pegged for a fool! You said you didn't care what happened to her."

"I've changed my mind."

Ives was dumbfounded.

Dave went on quietly, "That's one reason for keeping my word. Another is that if I don't buy Chevron for you, you'll do it yourself. When Gove understands he'll run Buckley and chase you out of the country or kill you. So I'll stick."

"You can't do it!" Ives said flatly.

Dave only smiled and looked at Pete Framm. "You want to buy in on this, Pete?"

"I've bought," Pete said soberly.

"And you, Martha?"

"I've bought, too," Martha Macy said quietly. She looked at Pete and smiled fleetingly.

Dave stood up. To Ives there was a quiet confidence about him that was better than a drink of Con's Irish whiskey. He watched Dave lift the six-gun from his waistband and study it, a faint, amused smile on his face. Dave glanced at Ives and said, "Chance's?"

"Likely."

Dave rammed the gun back in his waistband and then looked at the three of them. "If they're after me we'd better haul out of this camp. Martha, you spoke of the shack where you and Tip lived. Where is it?"

"Over   by   the   reservation,   south-east of Vermillion."

"That's our meeting place," Dave said. "Pete, you and Martha better line for it tonight. I'll pick up Ives tomorrow and meet you, and then we'll have a look at Seco camp."

To Ives he said, "Where does Con sleep?"

"Over his saloon. There's a back stairs."

Pete said soberly, "I'm pretty good at holdin' a horse in the dark, Dave."

"Not tonight."

Dave raised a hand and went out into the darkness.

Ives watched him go, and when he was gone Ives tried to recall what Dave had said that made him believe the plan was possible. He couldn't recall one concrete fact; there was nothing, except a kind of calm, dogged insistence that he could dodge a bunch of angry men under an implacable sheriff to talk with a girl who had every reason in the world to despise him.

Pete, watching Ives's expression, said gently, "He makes pretty big tracks, old-timer."

"That big?" Ives asked seriously.

Pete just nodded.

CHAPTER 12

Dave had his look from the canyon rim above Hilliard, and what he saw below puzzled him. The Olympus was dark, and there were only a few windows lighted in the hotel. The tie rails were empty, and Rollins' store was dark. From seventy feet above town he could barely make out the lone street below him. This wasn't the fever of preparation that Ives had implied. Had the posse left already?

A deep hard-bought knowledge of trouble told him to go slowly and look the town over carefully again. He was going down; that he knew. For if Gove had timed this all so well, then he would not stop now. What he wanted was Chevron, and quickly, and he would try to get it quickly. If Beth Hilliard believed Dave guilty of Seegrist's murder her revulsion against him would put her in the frame of mind to sell Chevron to Gove. Dave didn't believe she would, and he wondered at the faith he had in this girl. He had to make sure, though.

He circled back to the wagon road and put his horse down the grade into town. Even the stable was dark, the usual night hostler's lantern absent. He put his horse across the road and down into the Little Dun and slowly walked him upstream until he was behind the Olympus.

He dismounted on the bank and led the horse up it and haltered him on the ash-strewn shelf of earth between the stream and the saloon's back door. The outside stairway to the half story above the barroom lay beyond the door, and he mounted it slowly, putting his weight down gently on each step.

At the door at the head of the stairs he hesitated, hand on knob. Then he stepped inside quickly.

"Who's that?" Buckley asked.

"Wallace."

A match wiped across the floor and flared up, and Dave saw Con Buckley, reared up on one elbow, holding the match above his head. Con's great bulk was turned sideways in his sagging bed. He was lying atop the blankets, his shirt off and his massive arms almost splitting the seams of his underwear shirt.

When he saw it was really Dave alarm leaped into his face. He heaved himself to a sitting position and plucked the chimney off the lamp on the table by his bedside. When he'd lighted the lamp he said in a low voice, "How quick can you get out of here?"

"I'm here to see Beth Hilliard."

Con said dryly, "The hotel's jammed to the roof with the gang beatin' the brush up from Vermillion. My barroom is sleepin' fifteen on the floor. Kinsley's at the hotel, and the town's so mad he had to close my saloon to keep away from the booze."

"Gove in town?"

Con nodded.

"Then I've got to see Beth Hilliard."

Con said, half in anger, "Are you deaf? You can't do it. She's in the hotel."

"What room?"

Con swore blisteringly, and Dave waited him out with a deep patience. Con ended bitterly, "You're crowdin' your luck even bein' in the country."

"Ives said you'd help me," Dave prodded.

"Help you," Con said in a low tone. "Hell, does Ives think I can raise the dead? I can kill you, all right, if I let you go near the hotel."

Dave said in a faintly hostile voice, "You backed your play with fifteen thousand dollars, Buckley. And I'm liable to queer it for you unless I know if Beth Hilliard believes I killed Seegrist. If she does she'll sell out tomorrow to Gove."

Buckley regarded him in silence, seeing the

truth in what he said. He said morosely, "I talked to her and tried to pin her down. But I couldn't without making her and Gove suspicious."

"You see, I've got to find out."

Con rubbed his bald head fretfully and stared at the lamp, a deep pessimism in his face. He glanced at Dave then and sighed. "All right."

"Where's her room?"

"The first one off the head of the stairs. What can I do to help you?"

"Nothing."

"Yeah, nothin'," Con said softly, bitterly. He looked at Dave now, his eyes sad. "I'm an old man, Wallace, and I'm fat and afraid. I'm lettin' you do what I ought to be doin', and then I tell you you can't do it." He shook his head slowly, and his great jowls swung back and forth. "There was a time," he said bleakly, "when I'd have stood up to Gove and fought him. But I'm too fat, too old." He looked up at Dave. "I won't hold you to it, Dave. Ives won't either. But you're goin', aren't you?"

Dave nodded.

"Well, good luck, son." Con sighed.

Dave stepped out into the night and descended the stairs. He left his horse where it was, afraid now that in moving him he might rouse the curiosity of some light-sleeping posseman in the Olympus. Following the shelf of the riverbank around to the bend and the street, he paused in the shadow of the warehouse. The dark hotel was directly opposite.

In there, so Con said, were the men who would start the hunt for him tomorrow. One mismove and the powder keg would blow up in his face.

Standing there in the dark, he recalled Con's last words to him. Neither Con nor Ives held him to his bargain, and he still was going on. He could, as he had half pretended he was doing, make it a point of honor, but it wasn't that. Neither was it stubbornness, nor an obsession. Part of it was hating Chance and Gove, but the most of it was Beth Hilliard. At first her loyalty to Gove had seemed to him only a fool's blindness, but now it was something else again. He was seeing a woman whose character was breaking her, whose loyalty was betraying her, and he could not desert her now.

He had a moment of cold doubt and then crossed the deserted street and paused at the foot of the steps. The thing to do was go in boldly, though not noisily, and trust to the darkness to cover his identity.

He mounted the steps carefully and paused at the lobby door and peered into the darkness. As his sight became accustomed to the darkness he could make out the dark figures of men sleeping on the lobby floor.

Slowly, then, he picked his way among them, heading for the stairs.

And then a man whispered: "That you, Barney?"

Dave halted, and he did not dare answer the man. Yet if he didn't the man might give the alarm.

He whispered, "Which room's Kinsley in?"

"Second down. Any news?"

Dave grunted a negative and went on, and his questioner was satisfied. He climbed the stairs noiselessly and was in the corridor. The lamp in the wall bracket burned dimly, and Dave looked to his left and saw the door of Beth's room.

Debating a moment as to whether or not to risk a knock, he decided against it because of Kinsley next door. Slowly he opened the door. He stepped inside, closing the door behind him, and wiped a match alight on the wall.

Holding it overhead, he peered in the direction of the bed.

And there, her chestnut hair spreading thickly over her shoulders, was Beth Hilliard — awake, on one elbow, a cocked six-gun in her hand pointing at him.

Dave said quietly, "Don't be afraid. I want to talk to you."

"Don't light another match until I tell you," Beth said swiftly.

Dave dropped the match and stood there in the dark. He heard the bedsprings creak and the whisper of cloth on cloth.

Then a match came alight, and Beth, a blue wrap around her, her long chestnut hair gathered loosely at the base of her neck, lighted the lamp.

Then she turned and looked at Dave, and there was a real fright in her face.

"Don't you know this place is full of men hunting you?" she whispered.

Dave nodded and came over toward her. She sank down on the bed, staring at him, baffled by his calmness. In that instant there was something young and trusting in her face, and Dave knew with a quiet pride that she was not afraid of him. It was the answer to his question.

"But you can't stay here! You've got to go!" Beth said in excitement.

"After a couple of questions. You think I killed Seegrist?"

"No," Beth said immediately. "I know you didn't, Dave."

"Then who did?"

"I don't know."

Dave reached into his shirt pocket and took out the note he'd found in the gun. He unfolded it and extended it and said, "Last night in jail somebody slipped a gun to me. That note was in it. Recognize the writing?"

Beth glanced at it and looked up at him and said, "Last night? But Seegrist was killed tonight."

"That's right," Dave murmured. "They wanted me out so they could hang his killing on me. They knew I'd break jail if I had a gun and thought Seegrist was dead."

"They?" Beth asked. "You keep saying 'they.'"

Dave said dryly, "You don't like to hear his real name."

"You mean Jess?"

Dave nodded.

Beth wasn't angry now. She said with quiet patience. "You're wrong, Dave, terribly wrong. You're saying he killed one of his own crew. Why would he?"

"To hang it on me."

"And why does he want to?"

"To run me out of the country."

"And why would he want to do that?"

"Because I wasn't satisfied with his explanation of Tip Macy's death." Dave almost smiled. "We're right back where we left off, you see."

"I want to go beyond that," Beth said stoutly. "You're not satisfied that Tip was a rustler. Then why was he killed?"

"He'd found something that he wasn't meant to."

"About Jess?"

Dave nodded.

"What was it then?"

"When I find that I'll have Gove in jail," Dave said grimly.

Beth shook her head. "You're wrong, Dave. You can't give a reason for Jess killing Tip. There's nothing he wants."

"He wanted to keep me from Martha Macy so bad that when Chance found out I'd talked to her he was set to beat her into telling him what she'd told me."

Beth just stared at him. "When did this happen?" she asked slowly.

"Tonight. Young Pete Framm stopped it and took a licking from Chance. Martha Macy's left Chevron."

Beth came slowly to her feet, her gaze steady on Dave's face. "Are you sure of that?"

"When you get to Chevron you'll find out," Dave murmured. "Something else you'll find. I'm so sure you'll find it I'll make a bet with you."

Beth was silent, listening carefully.

"You'll ask about Martha. Gove will tell you" – he paused, his eyes sardonic, musing – "I'll make a guess what he'll tell you. He'll say Martha Macy's not a good woman. He'll say Chance saw Pete Framm and Martha Macy together, and he learned that every time nobody was at the place Martha would ask Pete into the house. He'll likely say Chance whipped Pete, and Martha left with Pete rather than be separated from him."

Beth's face showed a distaste now. She said quietly, "How cynical you are."

"I am about Gove," Dave agreed.

"And yet he'll be your partner," Beth said. "Have you thought of that?"

"Does that mean you still aim to sell Chevron to me?"

"I promised you I would and I won't back down." She added, almost with irony, "Don't mistake me. It's money I want. If I'm offered more from somebody else I'll take it."

"I'll have the money in less than a week," Dave replied.

"And you'll be Jess' partner," Beth repeated. "Have you thought of that?"

Dave regarded her closely with quiet somberness. "I've thought of this much of it. You'll be against me then."

Beth seemed troubled. "But I'm not against you now, Dave."

"You'll have to choose," Dave pointed out quietly. "It'll be either me or Gove."

Beth looked at him searchingly, her hazel eyes sober and almost pleading. "I suppose I will," she said slowly.

"The showdown will come."

"Don't be so hard on me, Dave!" Beth cried

in a low voice. She stood straight now, facing him. "Don't you see what you've done? All my life I've loved Jess Gove, and now you tell me that he's a fraud. I wouldn't believe anyone else who said that, but somehow I think — I don't know — you almost make me believe you. You're a strange, hard man, Dave. You've made me admire you; you've made me believe you in some things; you've made Sam Kinsley look a fool to me. You're changing my whole life, whether you know it or not!"

She stopped abruptly, almost in tears.

Dave was shocked into muteness, and he remembered again, this time with deep shame, his bargain with Ives. For a moment he was perversely proud that she was loyal to Gove. The fact that he'd tried in every way to break her loyalty and had at last cracked it now filled him with a humility that puzzled him.

Dave said gently, "I'm only trying to keep you from being hurt, Beth. Try to remember that."

"But why should you? We began this as quarreling strangers."

"Someday," Dave said slowly, "I'll tell you, Beth. I'll tell you how I started this and why I changed."

Beth said softly, "What do you mean, Dave?"

She was intent on his words when the knock came on the door. It was a soft, firm knock.

210

Dave remained motionless a part of a second, his head turned toward the door, and when he looked back at Beth the alarm was already in her face.

The knock came again.

Dave backed toward the wall and nodded to Beth.

"Yes?" Beth called.

"Who's in there with you, Beth?"

It was Kinsley . . .

The dismay on Beth's face was complete. Dave had the cold dismal feeling that the showdown was here, and he was in a bad spot. He couldn't fight it out, with Beth Hilliard in the same room with him. All he could do was hide and trust to the girl to bluff it out.

He glanced over and saw that he was on the wrong side of the door. If it opened he would be there for Kinsley to see.

He moved toward the door to get behind it, at the same time looking at Beth and motioning toward the door, then his lips.

Beth said steadily, "Nobody's here, Sam. Wait a minute."

And then the door flew open. Sam Kinsley, his face ugly with suspicion, stood there with his hand on the knob — not four feet from Dave, whom he'd caught in mid-step.

For one part of a second Kinsley stood there, dumbfounded. And in that second Dave acted.

He lunged, the whole force of his big body behind him, his only thought to get Kinsley out of the room before he could pull his gun.

His shoulder caught Kinsley full in the chest, and Kinsley's arms went up to grab the doorjamb. The savage driving impact of Dave tore his hands loose, and he gave a great grunt as the wind was driven from him. He tried desperately to get his balance, clubbing down on Dave's shoulder with his fist.

And then he was off balance as was Dave, too. Kinsley went backward into the stair well, clawing frantically at the wall, and then he disappeared.

Dave sprawled on his face on the very edge of the top step. He heard Kinsley land halfway down the steps with a crash that shook the building. Another crash came on the heels of the first, and Dave knew bleakly that the whole hotel would be roused. He came to his knees, looking down the hall, knowing only that this was a two-story building and that in a matter of seconds he would be trapped here. Again Kinsley crashed into the stairs, his boots racketing along the steps like a stick dragged on a picket fence. This time he yelled wildly.

Dave came to his feet, palmed up his gun, shot at the lamp in the wall bracket down the corridor, and then plunged down the steps in utter darkness.

There was a wild racket below now, and above it came Kinsley's enraged voice: "Wallace! It's Wallace!"

Dave jumped the last five steps. He landed on Kinsley, who rolled under him, and Dave went down.

The men sleeping in the lobby boiled out of their blankets, and as Dave rose to his knees one of them heading for the stairs, smashed into him, knocking him into a man just getting up.

Dave slashed wildly with his gun, intent on the door and his freedom. But it was a panic of yelling, fighting men, and above the clamor Kinsley's bull voice lifted in warning: "Don't shoot! Don't shoot!"

Dave could feel the terror in the room; it was something almost physical, and men were fighting each other blindly, half of them without knowing why.

A stunning blow caught Dave on the side of his head, and he went to his knees. A boot smashed down on his hand, grinding it into the floor, and he put his arms around the knees ahead of him and lifted and threw them forward.

Then he lay about him with his gun, slashing right and left, shoving, kicking, plunging toward the door. Some fool over by the stairs let off his gun in panic, and the bellow of it was deafening.

Dave saw a few of the wiser men dive through the door, but nobody yet had thought of a light.

Kinsley's bull voice was still yelling, timed like the pendulum of a clock. "Guard the bridge! Guard the bridge! Get a man on the bridge!"

Something butted into Dave's midriff then, and he rolled aside into another man, who cuffed him across the face with his palm. Dave struck out savagely with his gun and felt the sharp rap of it on somebody's skull. He took a step and put his foot on a man's back underneath him and then staggered into the man ahead of him, whom he shoved blindly toward the door.

The man went down, and now Dave saw the door ahead of him. He lunged for it, just as another man did. They wedged in the jamb, and Dave heard the timbers creak and groan. He raised his free arm and slugged at the man and shoved him under him and then crawled over and tripped and went sprawling on the porch into a chair, which splintered under his weight.

He clawed to the rail and vaulted it and dropped the eight feet to the ground, sprawling in the dirt.

A man on the bridge was yelling: "Cover the

grade. No, the grade! Cover the grade!"

Dave came to his knees, panting, and looked up and saw the men piling out of the Olympus. Three of them, hearing the man on the bridge, turned and ran for the grade at the opposite end of town.

Kneeling there, Dave knew he was trapped. Both roads out of town were bottled up, and it would be suicide to fight through these men, whose numbers were gaining by the second. And if he didn't get out they would search every building and room in this town until they found him.

He made his decision quickly, with no confidence at all, trusting blindly to chance.

Clinging to the side of the hotel, he went back toward the canyon slope, passed the end of the building, and started his climb. Behind him the racket in the hotel subsided. The Olympus was lighted now, and men were running down the street.

The talus slope of the canyon wall was not steep here, but that gave out in twenty feet, and now he was climbing naked rock. He worked with a sweating concentration, oblivious of what was going on below him now.

Slowly, slowly, he was mounting the face of the canyon wall, not knowing or caring how sheer it was, only content that he was making progress.

And then he felt his footing slip. He moved higher, lunging for a foothold, as the rotten rock beneath him gave way. He could hear it crumble and then break away and drop a short distance to the talus slope and start its roll. And then there was the sharp sound of boards splitting and breaking. Dave knew, without looking back, that a loosened boulder had rolled into the shed of the blacksmith shop.

He looked down now and saw the faces of the men in the street turned toward the canyon wall at the sound.

He glanced up and saw some ten feet above him, the rimrock dimly outlined against the night sky. The wall was sheer here, almost straight up, and its face so smooth that handholds were becoming scarce.

He held his breath, listening, working for a new handhold. He found one to the right of him and pulled himself up, clawing for a new foothold.

And then the man's bellow lifted into the night.

"There he is! Up by the rimrock!"

The first shot followed in a second and smashed into the rock way wide of him.

Doggedly, frantically, he searched for another handhold and found a crack in the rotting stone and pulled himself up two feet more.

The first gun was joined by another and then

by another. Dave heard the slugs slapping into the rock, showering splinters in his face, but he did not look back.

He looked at the rimrock, trying to will himself within reach of it.

A slug plucked at his trouser leg and ricocheted up past his head in a dismal whine. He heard men running, horses running, and still the shooting increased.

His blood was pounding in his ears, and he was fighting for a deep breath in his chest that panic had tightened ironhard.

And then he put his hands on the rim and clawed himself up and fell on his face and rolled away from the edge, and he heard the wild shouting and cursing below him.

He lay there a few seconds, dragging air into his tortured lungs, and then the pounding of a horse up on the rim to the south brought him to his feet, diving into the timber.

He let this horseman pass him as he clung to the dark and friendly hulk of a big pine. Others were coming. He plunged blindly into the timber, trusting the noise of his passage to be covered by the horses. When he was deep in it he stopped, listening.

The riders were beating the timber, back and forth, from the spot where he had climbed. He faded deeper into the trees, moving swiftly and silently, pausing to listen.

Then he saw the first lantern and he fled in the opposite direction. Pausing to listen now and then, he could hear the riders on all sides of him.

Half the men on the slope would be hunting him now, he knew. When they got organized they could spread out in a big circle and trap him. He must break through, south toward the grade, where he was close to Ives and a horse. And he must do it now, taking chances, before they organized.

He worked his way back toward the rim, falling back south, dodging from one tree to another, bolder now because he was desperate.

The riders coming off the road plunged blindly toward the spot where he had scaled the wall, and he kept the trees between himself and them. Now almost every rider had a lantern.

Dave worked constantly toward the road now. Once he was surprised by a trio returning, and the tree he had been driven to hide behind was not wide enough to cover him. He waited there, the riders passing within a dozen feet of him, and then on into the night without raising a cry.

He hit the wagon road presently and crossed it and stopped in the deep timber. Behind him he could hear the horses crashing brush, their riders calling to each other.

He walked swiftly, sometimes running, and

within half an hour walked into camp.

Ives had his fire doused, but he answered when Dave hailed him softly.

"You hurt?" Ives asked.

"No. You got a horse for me?"

"I'll dump the pack," Ives said.

In another five minutes, mounted bareback with a rope hackamore, Dave followed Ives into the night, and each minute put Hilliard farther behind him as they rode into black timber.

CHAPTER 13

It was sunup when Sam Kinsley returned to Hilliard for a change of horses. Beth, unable to sleep, had breakfasted after the last of the posse members, eating in relays, had finished their quick bite and ridden out. She had returned to her room through the wrecked lobby and paused to regard it. Every window in it was shattered; the corner desk had been righted again, but the lobby chairs were kindling. There was a big smear of ink on the floor where the desk had overturned, and in the gray morning light Beth shivered. She hoped unreasonably that Dave Wallace had escaped, but she didn't think it possible. He was afoot and these men were mounted, and the sober anger in their faces was warning.

She was in her room, gathering her few belongings, when she heard a heavy tramp on the stairs, and she knew instinctively it was Sam.

At the knock on her door she said, "Come in," and Sam Kinsley stepped into the room.

220

There was a smoldering anger in him; Beth could tell it by the set of his stubborn jaw. His coat was torn and dusty and sweat through, and a great welt was rising on his left cheekbone.

Shutting the door behind him, he said heavily, "I want to talk to you, Beth."

"I thought you would," Beth said. "Sit down, Sam."

Kinsley shook his head. "Haven't time." He was standing in the middle of the floor, his feet apart, and there was something almost frightening in the way he planted his thick body there, as if he were ready to fight.

"I don't like to do this, Beth," Sam said gravely. "But my job has some obligations."

"Sam, you're humorless," Beth said, smiling a little. "You don't need to impress me or explain. Just ask your questions."

"About Wallace."

"What do you want to know?"

"How he got here, for one thing."

"I think he came through the lobby. I can't be sure. He just stepped into my room and struck a match and there he was."

Sam looked at her steadily. "What did he want?"

"He wanted to know if I still planned to sell Chevron to him."

Sam's narrow lips curved down at the corners. "Does he think you're crazy?"

"He doesn't now, because I told him I'm selling to him, Sam."

A hot anger washed into Kinsley's eyes, and after the first moment of surprise he said incredulously, "Selling to him? Selling Chevron to Wallace after this? But why, Beth?"

"Money."

"You'd take a killer's money, then?"

"Not knowingly. But I don't think he's a killer, Sam."

"You know Seegrist is murdered," Sam said flatly, angrily.

Beth went over to the table and picked up the note Dave had left. She gave it to Kinsley, saying, "That note was in the gun that was smuggled to Wallace in jail. Seegrist was killed almost twenty-four hours later. Doesn't it seem to you that someone wanted to frame Wallace after he'd escaped?"

Kinsley read the note, looked bleakly at Beth, and crumpled the note in his fist. "You're very trusting, Beth," he said contemptuously. "All Wallace had to do to convince you was write a note and say he'd found it in a gun."

"I'm exactly as trusting as you are, Sam! All these men had to do to convince you Wallace killed Seegrist was just tell you he did!"

Kinsley was baffled and angry and, beyond that, surprised, too. "Beth," he said slowly, "I believe you're siding with Wallace."

"I am." Beth glared at him, wholly angry. "And while I'm about it, Sam. I don't like you walking in my room when you hear me talking to somebody."

"It was the middle of the night," Kinsley said accusingly.

"What business is it of yours who I talk to, or when!"

"Beth, Beth, what are you saying?" Kinsley said miserably.

"I'm saying you haven't any claim on me, Sam. You didn't know it was Wallace in my room last night. What right had you to break in like a — like a jealous husband?"

"I am a jealous husband," Kinsley said heavily, flatly. "I've told you, Beth, you're mine. And I'll protect you, as any man would his wife."

Beth felt sick with anger and humiliation. She was so furious that she really hated Sam Kinsley then. She tried to sort out the things she could say to him, but they were too weak, too impotent.

"Get out, Sam!" she said then. "Get out and stay out! You're a thick, clumsy bully of a man, and I don't want to talk to you any more."

"I'm the man you'll marry, all the same," Kinsley said quietly.

"You're the man I'll shoot if you don't leave!" Beth blazed.

He went out, and Beth sank down on the bed. She felt physically sick with anger and disgust at herself. Sam was mad, insane. Perhaps he's always been; only this time he was angry enough to speak his real mind. As she sat there a slow fear came over her. She had just looked into the mind and heart of a man who loved her and she was afraid of him. He was like some tamed and docile beast, who, once provoked, reverted to a fearful savagery.

There was a gentle knock on the door, and Jess Gove's voice came through the door. "Busy, Beth?"

"Come in, Jess."

Gove stepped into the room, his face benign and smooth-shaven and grave. The sight of him was comforting to Beth. Last night he'd swarmed out with the rest of them to hunt Wallace, and she hadn't had the chance to talk to him. But she knew just by looking at him that the hysteria of the man hunt hadn't touched him.

Jess looked sharply at her and sank into the chair. "What did you do to Sam? He's pretty ugly this morning."

Beth looked solemnly at Gove and said simply, "Jess, I'm afraid of him."

Gove looked surprised. "Why, Beth?"

"He just told me he considered me his wife and that he would protect me as his wife."

"What brought that on?" Gove asked gently.

"Wallace. Maybe you don't know what happened in this room last night, Jess. Wallace stepped in some time in the night and asked me if I still wanted to sell Chevron. I told him I did. When I told Sam about it he was almost insane with anger."

Gove nodded tolerantly. "He's tired, Beth — and mad, and he wants to break something. He's not accountable."

"But I've got a right to say what I think!" Beth said hotly. "I've a right to sell Chevron to the Indians if I want, and Sam can't stop me!"

"Of course you have."

Beth controlled herself then and took a deep breath. She stood up and walked to the window and looked out. She said, without turning, "I feel as if I'm in the wrong now, Jess. Do you think I am?"

"I think maybe you're a little hard on Sam," Jess said.

"I didn't mean that. I meant about selling Chevron."

"That's your own business, girl."

"I think so, too." She looked searchingly at Jess. "After all, Jess, you're the one who has the right to speak up. If I sell to Wallace he'll be your partner. You'd never accept a killer for a partner, Jess. I want to ask you again. Do you think Wallace killed Seegrist?"

"I do not," Jess said firmly.

"And you wouldn't mind him for a partner?"

Jess smiled tolerantly. "Beth, there's not an honest man in this world I can't get on with. And I think Wallace is honest. He's stubborn, but he's loyal and he's honest."

"Then I'll sell," Beth said, "because that's what I think, too." She turned away from the window. "Just give me a minute, Jess, and I'll be ready."

Jess rose, looking as if he wanted to say something. He started for the door and then paused and said. "Hang it, Beth. It doesn't get any better the longer it waits. I'd better tell you here."

Beth glanced up at him, surprised by the tone of seriousness in his voice.

"What is it, Jess?"

"It's about Martha," Jess said solemnly. "Chance told me this morning."

A kind of premonition froze Beth. She stammered, "Is — has anything happened to her?"

"She's gone," Jess said. He looked down at the hat in his hand and then raised his troubled glance to Beth. "This time I don't cover up by a white lie — not since Wallace caught me out." He hesitated. "This is no fit thing for you to hear."

"But what is it?"

Jess looked embarrassed. "Last evening Arnie

had just ridden out toward Pitchfork. He stopped to roll a smoke at the edge of the timber, and while he was doing it he saw young Pete Framm head for the house and go in."

Beth said nothing, waiting for the rest, knowing what it would be.

"He went back and" — Jess's glance avoided hers — "He found Martha and Pete together. Pete was fondling Martha — like he'd done it before. When Arnie faced them they admitted it." His face was suddenly stern now. "Chance kicked young Pete out. Martha chose to follow him, and she went with him." He paused and added, "I might say that I approve entirely of what Arnie did."

Beth did not speak, did not move. Gove shook his head and said, "I'm sorry to report that," and stepped out into the hall.

Beth was still as death. Last night Dave had predicted this, and now it had happened, almost word for word. If he was right about this he might be right about Jess all the way along.

With the thought of it, Beth knew real terror.

CHAPTER 14

It was dark when Ives and Dave rode into Tip Macy's place and dismounted. Pete came out to take their horses, not even asking the news. Dave and Ives walked stiffly toward the house, where Martha was waiting. Dave looked about him in the dark, almost knowing the kind of place this would be, because he had known Tip Macy's ways. The house was a two-room shack built of upended logs, sod-roofed. The corrals were of cedar poles, the sheds roofed with brush. It would be the spread of a small cattleman – poor, simple, and neat.

Martha left the stove to greet them and show them where to wash, and afterward they went in to the table and ate. When Pete came in Dave, still eating, told them what had happened at Hilliard and of his talk with Beth. When he came to the place in his story where Kinsley broke in he saw Martha smile faintly, enigmatically.

When he had finished eating and had rolled a smoke and lighted it he looked at Pete and

228

grinned. "Ready to travel?"

"Travel? You got to sleep," Pete said soberly.

"If we beat Gove to Seco tonight's the night."

Ives said grimly, "Right now," and rose. He and Pete headed out for the corral.

Dave rose and gathered an armful of dishes and carried them over to where Martha was cleaning up. He looked around the room now, almost for the first time, noting its poverty and its neatness. Last night when he had sent Martha and Pete here because it seemed safe he had not remembered the associations it was sure to hold for Martha.

Now he said, "I'm pretty thick in some ways, Martha. I didn't think how it would be for you when I sent you here last night."

Martha smiled at him and shook her head. "That's finished, Dave. I feel like I'm making it up to Tip now." She watched him clean the table of dishes, carrying them awkwardly, his big hands gentle with the few pieces of china she owned.

She said gravely, "Dave, you mustn't think too badly of Beth. She's no fool."

Dave stopped, his hands full of dishes, and looked at her. "I know that."

"I wasn't sure if you did." She shook her head slightly. "Do you remember when you talked to me up there at Chevron? I couldn't see your face, only hear you. And your voice shamed me for not being loyal to Tip. Remember?"

Dave nodded.

"Then don't hate Beth for her loyalty to Gove." She paused, and Dave nodded, soberly, and then she spoke again. "And don't think Sam Kinsley owns her, Dave."

Dave made his face expressionless, but he was listening carefully. In his eyes was polite query.

"I know what you thought," Martha said. "You wondered how Kinsley would dare break into her room without her permission."

"I did," Dave confessed.

"He loves her and he thinks that gives him the rights of ownership. When Beth left for the East he followed her for three days, ordering her to come back."

"And she didn't?"

"No. Beth Hilliard can't be bullied."

Ives stepped inside the door now and said, "Martha, what guns you got here?"

Dave found himself following Martha into the bedroom, where she kept the guns, but he was thinking of what Martha had just told him. In some obscure way what she had said comforted him. For all during the day he had wondered at Kinsley breaking in Beth's room last night. Dave hadn't forgotten the look of ugly suspicion on Kinsley's face, and it had troubled him. He'd been too proud to ask Ives, and Martha might have sensed that.

Martha brought out two rifles, a worn Colt .45, and shells for all three, and they took them and tramped out.

Pete had three horses saddled. He had exchanged Dave's horse for one of his own string that Martha had ridden down from Chevron, a deep-chested, short-coupled bay gelding.

They mounted and lined out abreast into the night, heading west toward the desert. With food inside him, Dave felt his sleeplessness hit him. He had been in the saddle almost two days and a night, and he was hungry for sleep. But Gove was not the kind to wait. After they saw Seco he could sleep.

He wondered idly what the Seco line camp would hold for them. Seco meant "dry" in Spanish, and Ives, discussing it during the day's ride, had said it was close to the desert. Aside from that, he knew nothing and could guess nothing. Inside the shack would there be signs that told of the fight in which Tip was killed? He doubted it. Yet there was something there that Chance and Gove had fought desperately to conceal.

It was long after midnight, and they were in a gently rolling country of thick grama grass that swished against the legs of their horses at every step; the black squat shape of an occasional cedar loomed and faded into the night as they rode. Off to the south was the vast spread of reservation grassland, while to the west lay the big and silent desert. Some of the loneliness of both was on this land, and Dave understood why Tip had settled here.

Ives reined up presently and pointed ahead into the night.

"It's about a mile yonder, set up above a dry arroyo. We go careful from here on, so leave your horses."

He led off, Dave falling in behind him. The land sloped gently now, and the scrub cedar was thicker. Presently Ives reined up and dismounted and went on afoot.

And then he hauled up so abruptly that Dave moved into him.

Dave looked ahead, and there at the bottom of the slope lay the crude line shack, naked to the starlight. There was a lantern lighted inside it.

Ives said grimly, "He beat us."

Dave looked carefully at the shack, and Ives faded silently into the night. There was a pole corral between the shack and the sandy bed of the dry arroyo, and the buildings squatted there in the starlight, barren of any surrounding trees. Dave knew now he had part of the answer. If this place wasn't important to Gove, why would these men be here?

Ives returned soon and said sourly. "Four

Chevron horses in the corral. It's Chance, all right."

Dave said nothing.

Ives murmured quietly, "I can go down. I can take a look, and they won't suspect me."

"It's not the shack," Dave said.

Pete looked at him in the dark. "Why not? Chevron hasn't had a man here this spring until now."

"If it was anything a man could see Chance would have burned the place," Dave said. He was quiet a moment. "It's the country, something here, something around here. And it's still here or Chance wouldn't be here now."

"But there's nothin' here except a holdin' corral. There's grass all around it, and behind it's the desert," Pete said.

"Something happened here that Tip Macy saw. It's still here," Dave reiterated stubbornly.

"How you goin' to look, though?" Ives demanded.

Dave was silent then, eying the shack through the night. The plan was slowly forming, and even now Dave knew what he would have to do.

He said quietly, "Ives, if I toll this crew away from here can you get your look?"

Ives said sourly, "You can't, without gettin' them on your neck."

"That's my idea."

He let Ives consider this for a moment in stunned silence and then he said, "As far as Chance knows, I'm alone. If he figures he can run me down and nail up my hide he'll pull the whole crew away from here and put them on me. When they're gone you step in."

"They spot you and they'll have the whole slope on your trail."

"But you can have your look, can't you?"

Ives said, "Yes," with a quiet, shrinking reluctance.

Dave turned to Pete. "You're free to ride this country, Pete. I'll need grub cached and a change of horses."

Ives cut in, and his voice was dead earnest: "Son this won't work. They'll crowd you into the high country and trap you in one of them canyons on up above. You don't know the country and they do. Once they got you on the run, instead of holed up, you're a gone goose."

"Maybe," Dave said quietly.

"You aim to go through with it?"

"If you two will back up my hand."

Pete answered instantly, as Dave knew he would. Ives was quiet for several minutes, sizing up the odds. Not for himself, but for his partner. Finally Ives said, "I don't like it, Dave. But it's your say."

"It's settled then."

They moved away from the shack, and in the

darkness, well away from the wash, they discussed their plans.

Afterward they broke up, Pete to return to Martha's place, Ives to cache himself where he could watch what went on at the shack, and Dave to return to the spot where they had first beheld Seco camp.

Dave took a rifle and all the shells for it Martha had given them.

When he drifted into the shadow of the cedar and looked down on the shack the lantern had been doused, and the men were sleeping.

He bellied down, his rifle by his side, folded his arms, and went instantly to sleep.

At dawn he wakened, chilled and stiff, and glanced at the east. The time was right now, for they could see him soon.

He levered a shell into his carbine, changed his position a little so as to be in better cover from the cedar, drew a bead on the shack's lone window, and fired.

The morning stillness was shattered by the sharp slap of the rifleshot.

He waited.

A Chevron hand, in his sock feet, appeared in the doorway.

Dave sighted on him, moved off, and fired again. The puncher dived inside, slamming the door shut behind him. Dave poured four shots into the door, moved to the window again, and emptied his rifle.

Now he reloaded, waiting. A rifle poked tentatively out of the window, and quickly Dave sent another shot at it.

Now he crawled back until he was out of sight, came to his feet, and moved downhill toward the arroyo. A single rifleshot came from the house, and when it was not answered three more guns joined in the clamor.

Dave dropped down into the arroyo, moved toward the shack. He picked a new position behind the bank and saw Arnie Chance standing uneasily in the door of the shack.

Again Dave shot, and this time he saw a splinter of wood fly off the door where his bullet had struck. Chance vanished.

Leisurely, then, Dave put some shots into the window and then again at the door, until it was finally closed and barred. He knocked the stovepipe off the roof and then started searching with his slugs for the chinks in the logs.

Pausing between shots now, he could hear a man's vicious cursing inside the shack. Finishing out that load, he moved again, this time to the other side of the shack, and again he opened up. Nobody tried to run out; he had a dry, ironic smile as he pictured the inside of the shack, with the crew lying on the floor, helpless, swearing, their nerves wire-edged with wondering when some lucky shot might hit them.

When he had exhausted his shells he threw the rifle aside and retreated in the chill dawn to his horse. Mounting, he put him toward the mountains, starting off at a long lope.

Two hours later he pulled up on a rise of the foothills, dismounted, and took a long look at the country he had just passed through. In the light of the low morning sun he could see the long tawny stretches of rolling country that finally, in the dim distance, gave onto the desert. Trees stood out sharply, and he patiently studied his back trail. Off on the wagon road from the agency, connecting with the Hilliard-Vermillion road, he saw a funnel of dust that indicated a rider with his horse at a dead run. That could be Chance's messenger to the posse. Closer now, he was patiently studying the country when, scarcely a mile away, he saw three riders top a rise. They were spread out, coming fast, following the tracks he had not bothered to disguise.

Dave quickly stepped into the saddle now and headed into the foothills. It was Chance, all right, and if the rider he had spotted on the distant road was Chance's messenger, then it meant the Seco camp was abandoned.

When he reached the timber Dave angled off south, rode steadily for a half-hour, and then turned north, still climbing.

When after twenty minutes he pulled up to breathe his horse he turned in the saddle and listened.

And then he heard distinctly, from no great distance, a man calling to his partner.

Dave's face hardened with a sudden alertness, and he almost smiled. Chance was good at this. He was crowding him hard, playing his hunches.

Dave put his bay into the timber again now. Chance's hunches were no good unless the man he was hunting knew the country and Chance could anticipate his moves. Dave, realizing this, settled down to the hard business of trying to shake his pursuers. He climbed, almost steadily, until he was in a country of rock outcropping, and then he got to work. He traveled swiftly, then moving from one outcrop of rock to another, never bothering to be careful, but just cautious enough to slow down Chance and his men if they were hunting his tracks.

When he worked thus for an hour or so he took his chance and cut downslope, reasoning that Chance would have to draw his two men in to help pick up the tracks in the rock outcrops.

He traveled carefully now, watching, his pace slow.

Coming to a small meadow, he paused, looked it over, and started across. He was only yards into it when he heard underbrush snapping in the timber at the far edge of the meadow.

He reined his bay around and put him swiftly back into the timber and up the slope, angling north again now. It was only a few minutes before he heard a gunshot, and he knew that the rider had picked up his fresh trail and was summoning help.

And then he heard five answering shots, all behind him and widely scattered.

He knew now that Chance's help had arrived already. By nightfall it would be doubled or tripled.

Climbing steadily now, he looked at the sun and judged he had five hours more until dark. His horse was tiring, and this was strange country. He gave up all thought now of turning downslope in the daylight hours. He centered his attention on skirting the canyons which became more frequent as his course climbed.

Coming to a trail at a canyon mouth, he picked it up and followed it, reasoning that it would take him into yet higher country. Occasionally he heard shots behind him, always at the same distance, it seemed to him.

He was climbing out of the canyon soon, mounting steadily on a narrow trail on the south face.

He heard the slap of the slug on the stone face of the wall beside him before the report of the rifle boomed out into the hot afternoon stillness.

Some one had spotted him from across the opposite rim of the canyon. He did not hesitate a second but roweled his horse, leaning across the bay's neck. If he turned back it would be into the arms of the men following. He chose the long stretch of climbing trail ahead.

The next shot put a sharp rock splinter in his cheek, and he cursed quietly, sweating, talking to his horse, urging him. The big bay was bone-weary, but he was fighting. And the timber was close ahead now.

The third and fourth and fifth shots were wide, as the marksman saw himself crowded for time. And then Dave plunged into the timber and reined up, breathing his bay for a precious few seconds.

The shots, he knew, would summon the whole pack of them below. And even now the marksman would be trying to cut him off ahead.

Dave turned into the timber then, but instead of losing himself in it, he clung as close to the rim as he could, riding in the direction from which the shots had come. He rode slowly, almost holding his breath, his senses straining for the first warning sound.

He pulled up abruptly, listening. Off to his right in the underbrush he heard a horse slashing through it at a dead run that was almost suicidal in its headlong rush. He stayed quiet as death, and when the sound dimmed in the distance he put the bay ahead once more.

This was a reprieve that might last until dark, he thought.

It did not.

An hour later he came into a big clearing and saw on the far side of it five men dismounted, their horses watering at a spring seep. Below them a pair of shots lifted into the warm afternoon, and one of the riders pulled his gun and answered.

Automatically Dave pulled his weary horse back into the screening timber and headed up the slope again. Ives had been right this time too. They were crowding him into the high country where, one by one, his chances of escaping or even of hiding were cut down hourly.

In a thick stand of spruce above the clearing he let his horse have another breather, and he looked desperately at the sun that was heeling over to the west with a maddening slowness. Later, angling north, he came to a trail and spent several precious minutes hunting for a rock face on which to cross it. If the crew in the clearing were sharp enough the end of the search was only an hour off. For his horse was close to done and could not stand another spurt of chase. He himself was dozing in the saddle.

He listened then, and when twenty minutes passed and he had not heard shots he knew he was behind the first line of the pursuers.

He clung to deep timber, barely moving, listening constantly, until the dark curtain of dusk thickened the twilight of the timber. When it was full he slid out of the saddle, stretched, and led his horse to a small creek that he had kept on his right for the past hour. He was almost asleep on his feet.

Afterward he mounted and set out again, heading downslope, this time in the black night. The descent would be even harder on his spent horse than the climb had been, but he steeled himself against pity. If he didn't get through tonight into lower country he was done for.

The descent, he soon found, would be fantastically difficult. The canyon trail where he had been shot at this afternoon had put him on a bench which ran north and south and had only trails down from it. These trails, he knew, would be watched. Chance and his men and the others had succeeded in moving him onto this bench in one day, and they would not let him turn back in the night.

In the dark, after an hour of fruitless search in which time and again his bay would stop and refuse to take the steep slopes ahead of him, Dave was baffled. He was dozing in his saddle, his mind thick and uncaring with the need for sleep, yet he knew that if he gave in and slept he was done for tomorrow.

He flagged his mind into wakefulness and took desperate stock. He couldn't find a trail down in this darkness, nor could he crowd his almost foundered bay into taking a slope in the dark which might result in crippling him. Nor could he stay on this bench. There was one alternative remaining, and he chose it immediately in desperation.

He followed the rim until, through the trees, he saw the distant light of a campfire. Dismounting, he moved toward it through the timber until he was close enough to observe it.

There were five men here, three of them rolled in their blankets by the fire. The other two were on watch, talking in low voices. The fire, Dave saw, was built square on the trail off the shoulder of a big boulder.

On the other side of the fire it was pitch-black, and Dave guessed that a sharp drop was there. The horses stood between him and the camp.

He went back to his bay, mounted, and considered all this a still, sleepy moment, and then he put his horse into motion.

As quietly as he could he moved in toward the hobbled horses on picket. One of them wickered nervously, and Dave cursed him silently. The men at the fire looked up and then returned to their talk.

He wondered dismally if his bay would rebel at moving away from these horses. Perhaps in fear of this he roweled him with a savage pressure. The bay shied wildly, and Dave jerked him back into the trail, heading for the fire. The men at the fire, hearing the racket, started to rise. And then Dave palmed his gun up and shot and rode down on the camp.

He kneed his horse straight at the pair of punchers. One of them swung his rifle up and fired blindly at the noise, and then Dave was on them. They leaped aside, and one of the sleepers, roused by the shots, reared up in front of the bay. The horse swerved and then jumped the fire, and one of the guards, flattened against the boulder, let off his six-gun almost in the bay's face. His shot was pure panic. The bay, sensing the drop on the far side of the trail, hugged the boulder, nevertheless, and his shoulder caught the puncher in the chest and slammed him against the rock. The rifleman let go then, the slug ricocheting off the boulder into the night over Dave's head.

And then he was on the trail, the horse frantically checking its speed because the firelight had blinded him.

Dave gave him his head, listening to the

uproar behind him. The whole camp opened up now, but they were shooting in the dark.

Dave let the bay take his time, and when he was in the canyon bottom he looked back. The first horse of the pursuers was taking the trail now.

Dave put his bay into a walk again, and again let him have his head. Now he fought to keep awake and could not. He dozed a half-dozen times and came awake to listen and doze while he was listening.

At last, an hour later, the bay sighed and came to a halt. When Dave wakened the bay was standing patiently, trembling with weariness.

Dave slipped out of the saddle, fell, and when he found he was on a soft cushion of pine needles he did not move. He slept that way, dead to the night and everything else.

CHAPTER 15

Ives waited until an hour past dawn, long after Dave's shooting was finished, and then approached the shack boldly, as he always did in his wanderings. His casualness was wasted; the camp was deserted.

Swiftly, then, Ives set about his search. He examined the inside of the shack carefully, but he did not know what he was looking for. It was like any other line shack — dirty, crude, smelling of grease and sweaty clothes and leather. There was nothing in here to excite a man's suspicion, and Ives went outside. Remembering Dave's insistence that what they were looking for was somewhere around here, he tried to view this line camp as it might be described to a stranger.

It was a dry camp, with no water. The reason for its existence was simple enough. In storms and dirty weather the crew who pushed the drifting cattle back from the rim made this their shelter. Too, there was a trail down off the rim into the desert, he remembered. It was closed with a brush fence, to keep cattle from straying down onto the desert in storms. And then he thought about Tip Macy. Martha had said he was headed for Seco camp — presumably because in the blizzards the cattle might drift off the rim or down into the desert. Something happened here during the blizzards — and that, obviously, was connected with the rim or the desert. Reasoning thus, Ives went over to his mare and stepped in the saddle. He was going to have his look at the desert.

The trail which led off the rim was really the bed of the arroyo which, in the centuries of fast, cutting floods, had ground a channel through the soft red sandstone of the rim. Where it began to drop, cutting into the sandstone and forming walls, a thick cedar-brush fence had been lined across the fifty-foot expanse of arroyo. During each flood, of course, the fence went out and had to be replaced, so Ives placed no importance on the fact that the ax marks on the brush were relatively new.

He laboriously pulled a hole in the brush, led his horse through, mounted, and went on down the canyon. It dropped steeply, the crowding red walls mounting ever higher, and then twisted and turned and dived down the hundred feet of the rim until it came out on a high sandy delta of talus. It was rough going for a horse, but Ive's mare negotiated it. Before him now was the desert, and Ives reined up to look at it.

Ives didn't like the desert. He was a mountain man, and where there were no trees, no streams, no animals, he did not want to be. Vermillion Desert did not start abruptly. Sage and scattered rabbit brush grew at the base of the rim, but, stretching out into the distance, the growth slowly disappeared or was drifted over with blow sand. Beyond the deep desert lay bleaching in the sun — a waterless waste of sand and rock that Ives eyed sourly. A dry patch of country he could respect as an immutable law of nature. But the Vermillion was more than a patch: it was big, utterly waterless save for the foul seep of water at the two stage stops, and a small seasonal rain catch at the Bunchgrass Tanks. It was so vastly useless that Ives hated it. Nor was he alone in his dislike, for the Utes to the south shunned it, and the whites barely accepted it. One lone wagon road crossed it, rather than circle the five hundred miles around it north or south. Its black hills reared up in the far distance against the dazzling glare of its floor, and it reminded Ives of the bleached skeleton of some beast of prehistory too big and too ugly to contemplate.

He put his mare off the talus slope and rode along under the rim for a mile or so, his course aimless. What was he to look for? Tip Macy was killed because of something around here, but what was it?

Ives turned back, baffled. He looked out at the desert again. Now he saw something out among the brush-covered dunes, and he put his mare toward it. Approaching, he saw it was the skull and bones of a steer, bleached into a whiteness that almost hurt his eyes. He dismounted, could not estimate when it died, and gave up. Mounting, he pulled his mare around in disgust and headed back for the trail. This sun glare out here hurt his eyes, and he looked at the towering red cliffs with a sense of relief.

His glance fell to the desert floor, and he saw old cattle sign, bleached into grayness. There was a lot of it, some of it was drifted over with sand. He glanced away at the cliffs again, frowning, but now something he couldn't name was nagging at his mind.

And then he pulled up abruptly and looked again at the ground. Here was cattle sign again, lots of it.

And what was it doing down here on the desert floor?

Sitting motionless in his saddle, he looked around him and then walked his mare slowly back and forth. There was cattle sign all around him. Of course a few steers, like this dead one back there, were bound to break through the brush fence and drift down here, but not this many.

Why, according to the amount of this old sign, this was a driven herd.

And then it came to him. *This was what Chance was trying to hide!*

He sat motionless for a second, raw excitement holding him breathless.

Then he put his mare toward the trail. Where the delta of arroyo sand ended he stopped and walked his mare back and forth. Again the sign. It was under the drift sand that the wash had carried down. He followed the sign to its outer edge and then turned toward the desert. Now he followed the sign for a mile, and it headed straight into the desert.

Ives stopped then and looked out into the shimmery white sands of this big hell. Occasionally, ahead of him, he could pick out the bleached gray cattle sign heading still into the desert, and for a moment Ives doubted his sight.

The significance of this now slowly formed in his mind. A herd of cattle, coming down the trail, had headed into the waterless desert.

And then it clicked. *This was the herd of Chevron two-year-olds that Gove said had been winterkilled!*

Ives found himself expelling his breath slowly, a wild excitement in him. And then the doubt entered.

Hell, no herd could get across the waterless Vermillion. It couldn't be done; cattle needed water, and this country didn't have it. He remembered suddenly that during the worst storms this winter there had been some snow on the desert. But that would not last an hour in this thirsty sand after the storm.

Still, these tracks headed into the desert. To Ives that meant only one thing. There was water out there that Gove and only Gove knew about. He rejected that instantly as absurd, and yet there was nothing else to think.

Ives made up his mind with swift decision. He'd go look.

For a solid five minutes, the hot sun beating down on his shaved head, Ives sat there, thinking. He'd need a hat. He'd have to carry water and food, and to do it he'd need a pack horse. Which meant he must go back to Macy's place.

He pulled his mare around and headed for the wash, and now the excitement was steady.

At sundown Ives led his pack horse down the trail off the rim, and after covering his tracks as best he could he headed out into the desert. He got the direction in which this long-past herd had traveled, set his course by the stars, and traveled all night.

When daylight came he found himself in a fantastic county of upthrust hills of malpais and sand dunes and sun-blasted rock. As soon as he could see he turned at right angles, south, and started his search for the cattle sign. He found it on a stretch of rotten purple-colored rock that ran a barrier across this part of the desert for a few miles.

Satisfied, he hunted some shade in the over-hang of some malpais. He fed and watered his two horses from the kegs the pack horse carried, ate hastily, and rolled in for a hot and fitful sleep.

In late afternoon he started out again, heading deeper into the desert. He knew now that there was water out here, for this herd of cattle would not be driven two days out from water. That night he took his direction again, and again he traveled steadily until daylight.

When dawn came it seemed to Ives he was in a lost world. The Dun River Range had almost disappeared over the horizon, and the familiar landmarks were gone. To Ives this was a lost world. Nothing ever cooled off here. The rocks were almost as hot at dawn as they were at sundown, and he was hunting a thinning trail of cattle sign.

That morning he didn't find them. He cast south for miles and saw nothing, and then cut back north. Still no sign.

At midday the sun was broiling. Everywhere Ives looked the horizon shimmered in the heat waves, and the reflected light seemed to blast his eyes deep in his skull.

He paused now, squatting down in the brief shade afforded him by his mare and pondered the disappearance of all sign. He knew that if there was no sign here, then sometime in the night he had come beyond water. He must go back, casting about for the sign of the water.

He calculated how much water he had left, and he knew it was enough for today and tomorrow. When it was gone he must not be more than a day's travel from the rim.

He mounted and turned back, knowing that now in the daylight hours he couldn't sleep. He had to watch.

In midafternoon he had still not picked up the sign, and he was despairing. If he didn't find sign, then he was bound to find the skeletons of two thousand cattle who'd died of thirst, he reasoned.

He pulled up on the lip of rock shelf and looked ahead of him. A shallow swale in the dunes cut across his path, black rock and stony soil jutting out from the sand.

And then he spied something that aroused his curiosity. It was a lone Jimson weed, dead and dry, halfway up the opposite side of the swale. He stared at it, first because it was the only thing to look at, and then out of curiosity. Jimson, tough as it was, took some water. And there was no water here.

And then it came to him. This swale could have run water, just as an arroyo does. It was filled with blow sand, but nevertheless, he could make out its channel. If this Jimson were half grown, then it argued that water had been through here, and for long enough to give the weed half growth.

Ives eyed the swale, saw the grade was to the north, and put his horse into it, heading north, too, suspending judgment.

Three miles beyond the swale suddenly vanished, and Ives found himself in what seemed to be a dry lake bed. All around it were half-grown weeds, now dead and almost drifted over. Ives, in his excitement, deserted his pack horse and put his mare past the weeds, and there, above, he found the cattle sign again, thick.

It made swift, shocking sense now. With the heavy runoffs of the deep snow above the rim, the desert had actually run water. And the grade ended here in this lake, which might have held for two or three weeks. And as blizzard followed blizzard all through the winter and spring, Gove had driven his steers across to this lake where nobody dreamed there was water. It was perhaps halfway across the Vermillion Desert. From here across to the Bunchgrass Tanks was a shorter driver than from the rim to here. And from the Bunchgrass Tanks, which were full in the spring, to the Mesquite Hills was even less.

This accounted for Gove's two thousand head of winter-killed cattle.

They were stolen, and by Gove himself, because he'd tried to cover it up.

Ives sat there in the blasting sun, and in spite of it he shivered. This was the gentle, kindly Gove, Beth Hilliard's partner. He had ruined her, pretended ruin himself, and was now trying to salvage Chevron and the reservation lease for himself. For with the money he'd got from the stolen steers he could pay for the Indian grass and stock it.

It was freeze-out — with murder to enforce it. For the trail of these steers, driven out under the secrecy of one of the blizzards, was what Tip Macy had seen at Seco camp. And it was why he was murdered and moved to the boundary-line camp and his death made to look like a cattle thief's murder.

Ives sat there, stunned and shaking, while the murder built up in him.

CHAPTER 16

Nobody in Hilliard talked of anything but the man hunt. Its progress was reported at least twice a day, and Beth found herself running on needless errands to Rollins' store for news. Twice Beth had resolved to go home to Chevron, and twice she had changed her mind. It was the night after Dave had escaped when, lying sleepless in her dark room, she faced the real reason why she was unable to return to Chevron. It was because of Jess. His story of Martha's sordid affair with Pete Framm – the story that Dave Wallace had predicted Gove would tell – had shaken her. It was constantly in her mind, tormenting her, making her life miserable. For if Dave Wallace had been so right about that, he might be right about all the other things he'd said of Jess.

It was on the third noon after Dave's escape that Beth went into Rollins' store for her mail. Rollins was peering out through the wicket among the pigeonholes, intent on the story of a haggard-faced Star 33 rider. There were a half-dozen people gathered round him, listening, as Beth walked in.

The puncher was saying bitterly, "Sure they shot at him! But he was in the middle of a camp of five men before they was awake, and they was afraid to really cut down on him."

"He got away, then?" Rollins said.

The puncher nodded. "And he's headed downslope. I been ridin' all night to get here and raise a bunch to try and head him off. Who's around?"

Beth stepped forward then and with mild interest asked, "Is this Wallace who escaped?"

The puncher saw her and touched his hat and said, "That's right, Miss Hilliard. He's loose again."

Beth asked for her mail and went out. There was a feeling of relief, even elation, upon her that made her want to sing. She hurried back to the hotel and when she was inside her room she locked the door. She found that she'd been hoping against hope that they wouldn't get him, and now that he was safe for a while longer she was weak with relief.

Beyond that, however, Dave Wallace's escape had helped her to a decision. It had come reluctantly, and she was not proud of it, but it was the only way she would win a peace of mind. She was going to put Jess Gove to the test.

She sat down at the table, took a piece of paper and pencil, and practiced disguising her handwriting. When it had achieved a masculine carelessness that looked genuine she took a clean sheet of paper and wrote: DEAR MISS HILLIARD: *I will be at the second ford where Seegrist was shot from ten till midnight Thursday night with the money for Chevron. Yrs. obediently,* DAVE WALLACE.

She read it over, wondering if it was in character. Dave Wallace was not an educated man, but Beth knew he had had schooling. The flaw was that he would misspell. She recopied the note, writing "Thursdy" and "mony" and then, satisfied, put it in an envelope, sealed it, and addressed it to herself.

She waited until the paste on the envelope was dry, and then opened it and put it with her other mail.

Afterward she went down into the dining room. The room was empty, and she took a table by a side window and ordered her meal.

While she was waiting Tom Hyam came in. He crossed directly to her table. "Miss Hilliard, may I see you when you're finished eating?"

Beth said, "Sit down, please, you can see me now."

Hyam pulled a chair out and sat down, and Beth watching him, could not overcome a feeling of distrust for him. There was an arro-

gance in his face and an insolence in his eyes
that he did not bother to hide, even now.

"I hope you won't mind if I speak about this,"
Hyam began. He eyed her calmly, fingering a
piece of silverware. "It's common gossip in
town, so I'm not prying."

"What is it?"

"Have you promised to sell Chevron to Dave
Wallace?"

"The gossip is accurate for once," Beth said
quietly. "I am."

Hyam nodded. "I was in the lobby the day
Wallace made his offer. It was fifteen thousand
dollars. Is that the figure agreed upon?"

Beth nodded wonderingly.

"This is more gossip," Hyam said, smiling
faintly. "I understand you've said you'll sell
Chevron to the highest bidder."

"I will."

Hyam said quietly, "I'd like to bid two thousand five hundred higher than Wallace, then."

Beth just stared stupidly at him. She had a
sudden urge to laugh, but she stifled it. The
whole business of selling Chevron had reached
the realm of the fantastic. Gove's simple offer
of a thousand dollars had grown now to a
$17,500 offer from a dissipated gambler.

"Are you serious?" she asked.

"Dead serious."

Beth looked out the window, and a small

feeling of disappointment was in her. Was it because she had secretly hoped all along that Chevron would go to Wallace? Her rejection of that was swift and instantaneous. She had wanted to sell to Wallace only because he had offered more money. But self-deception was something Beth Hilliard had always denied herself and she knew this wasn't wholly true. Hyam was offering more money than Wallace, yet she did not want to sell to him, and she could not make herself give an answer.

And then a way out came to her, and she seized upon it without thought.

She looked at Hyam and said, "Whoever buys my share of Chevron will be a partner of Jess Gove. And I won't sell to a man he doesn't approve of as a partner."

Hyam smiled faintly. "That's hardly flattering, Miss Hilliard. You're suggesting I'm not as desirable a partner as a tough gunman."

"I didn't intend to be flattering," Beth said instantly.

Hyam said coolly, "You don't like me, do you, Miss Hilliard?"

"Frankly, I don't," Beth answered, just as coolly.

"Are your reasons private?"

"Not at all. I think you're a plain liar, Mr. Hyam. I don't think you saw Wallace near the second ford the day Seegrist's horse was shot."

Hyam's cynical face colored a little, "I think I'm the best judge of what I saw."

"And I think I'm the best judge of what I choose to believe," Beth retorted.

They were silent a moment, eyeing each other warily.

Hyam said finally, "Then you'll not sell to me?"

"It rests with Jess Gove. If he doesn't mind having you for a partner I'll sell to you."

Hyam rose and looked down at her. "Tell Gove I haven't many virtues, but one of them is that I don't shoot men when they're asleep."

He nodded insolently and walked out of the dining room.

When Beth's food came she was too distracted to eat. Hyam's insulting remarks weren't a quarter so disturbing as the revelation that she wanted Dave Wallace to have Chevron. Did she understand herself so little as all that?

She ate quickly and went back upstairs to her room. Inside, alone, she stood at the window, looking out over the drowsy town. She was restless and angry with herself and a little ashamed of herself too.

She was standing thus at the window when a knock came on her door and she answered, and Jess Gove came in. Sight of him brought Beth back to reality with a shock. She had forgotten the plans she had so carefully laid this morning.

Gove greeted her and came over to the window to stand beside her. There was a twinkle in his eye as he looked at her and said, "I've just been down to Rollins'."

"Did they tell you?"

Gove nodded. "Maybe I'm a renegade, Beth, but the news of Wallace's escape made me feel good. My partner seems to be taking care of himself."

Beth looked for the deceit in his words and found none. She said, "Can you stand a shock, Jess?"

He looked at her inquiringly.

"Hyam just offered me $17,500 for my share of Chevron."

She watched his face grow thoughtful, pensive.

"I told him it was up to you. I hinted that you wouldn't want him for a partner and that I'd not sell to him if you didn't."

Gove smiled faintly and squeezed her arm. "Bless you, Beth, but that's got nothing to do with it."

"It has everything to do with it."

Gove shook his head and walked across to the bed and sat on its edge, his shoulders stooped, his face thoughtful. He looked old and frail, then, and Beth knew a moment of doubt as she watched him.

"I've told you, Beth, I can get on with anyone in the world."

"Anyone honest, you said."

"And you don't think Hyam's honest?"

"I think he lied when he said he saw Wallace near the ford the day Ed was shot at."

"He could have been honestly mistaken."

Beth shook her head in negation. "You're too tolerant, Jess."

Gove said quietly, "If you're putting this up to me, Beth, I want you to take his offer."

"But, Jess, you —"

Gove held up a hand. "Listen to me, Beth. There's only one thing really close to my heart. That's what happens to you. I'm old and I've seen what money, or the lack of it, can do to a woman. It's the difference between misery and happiness, drudgery and contentment. Why, you can live a year, and well, on the difference between Wallace's and Hyam's offer. I can get along with either of them, so long as I know you're provided for." He paused and said gently in a low voice, "Believe me, Beth, that's true."

Beth turned to the window to hide her face. Jess's words flooded a scalding shame through her that she had ever doubted him. And then the memory of Dave Wallace's words rose in her mind — hard, sardonic, daring her to open her eyes. For long minutes she was torn between the two, and then, ashamed and sad, she made up her mind.

She went over to the stack of mail and drew out the note she had composed and silently handed it to Jess.

He read it slowly and then looked up at her.

"If I accept Hyam's offer I'll have to tell Wallace," Beth said.

"That would be only fair," Gove agreed.

"I'll tell him, then." Beth pretended to be thinking. "He'll be there at the second ford for two hours, Jess. Tomorrow night I'll wait until ten-thirty, when the hotel porch is clear and everybody's at the saloon. Then I'll ride up and tell him. I should make it by midnight easily if I ride hard."

Jess nodded. "I'll be almost sorry to miss having Wallace as my partner."

"One thing, Jess," Beth said gravely. "Promise me you won't even hint about our meeting tomorrow night to anyone."

"I promise," Jess said solemnly. "If the word got out he'd be captured. I'd hate to see that."

They talked for a little while, and then Gove left. Alone now, Beth began to regret what she'd done. How cheap she'd been to plan this shabby trap, just to learn if Jess was the glib liar Dave thought him! But it was too late to turn back now. If there was nobody at the ford tomorrow when she rode up it would prove that Dave was wrong about Jess Gove. It would prove Jess her trusted friend. She wondered if she could ever make up for doubting him.

In late afternoon Beth heard horsemen on the street and went to the window. More of the posse, dusty and tired and their horses sweating, rode down the street toward the feed stable for a change of mounts.

She went out now and headed for Rollins' store. Perhaps these men had fresh word of the hunt for Dave.

She was in front of the blacksmith shop when she saw Pete Framm step out of the barbershop ahead of her. His lean face was freshly shaven, and he paused on the step of the shop to roll a cigarette.

When he saw Beth his face reflected a subdued, almost shy pleasure. He touched his hat to her, and Beth smiled and said hello.

And then she stopped and faced him. "How's Martha, Pete?"

"All right," Pete said guardedly.

Beth could see that he was personally friendly to her but that he was being careful. It made what she had to say that much harder.

"Pete, Martha has talked to Dave Wallace, hasn't she? I know that, because Gove said she admitted it."

"Did he tell you what Chance did to her?" Pete asked thinly.

Beth shook her head. "Let's not quarrel,

Pete. I have a message for Dave Wallace. You can take it to Martha, and Martha can tell him."

"Wallace is on the dodge, so I hear," Pete said dryly.

Beth said stubbornly, "All the same, Pete, you tell her. I want to get word to Wallace if I can." She paused. Pete's face was alert, skeptical, polite. "She's to tell Wallace that I'm not selling Chevron to him. Hyam has offered me more money, and I'm accepting his offer."

Pete had been holding his half-rolled cigarette in his fingers. Now he looked down and carefully, studiously, finished fashioning his smoke before he glanced up at her.

"Maybe Wallace will raise his ante," Pete said mildly.

"I've thought of that. You can tell him that I won't sign with Hyam until I've got word from him. Can he get it to me?"

"I wouldn't know," Pete said carefully. Beth thought she saw a quiet relief in his eyes now.

"Will you tell her?"

"Yes'm," Pete promised.

Beth thanked him and walked on.

Pete waited until she had turned into Rollins' store, then he dropped his cigarette and headed for the tie rail and his horse.

CHAPTER 17

When Dave broke through the cordon of posse-men down to the low country Arnie Chance knew Seco camp was again threatened. He heard the news that morning and he saddled up, told his men curtly that he was going to see Gove, and rode straight for Seco camp. Arriving in the night, he circled the camp warily, made sure there was nobody there, and then slept in the shack till dawn.

At the first light by which he could see Chance went down to have his look at the brush fence.

It looked undisturbed, but Chance was a suspicious man. He patrolled it on both sides and saw nothing to disturb him. But it didn't satisfy him, and he pulled a hole in the fence and walked his horse through and mounted and went down the trail toward the desert.

On the talus slope behind he saw the tracks of Ives's horses, and his suspicions were confirmed. He studied the tracks bleakly and then raised his bleached eyes to the desert. Afterward he followed the tracks patiently, wondering at the aimless course, until he came to where Ives had dismounted to look at the skeleton of the steer.

And there, in the sandy soil, Chance saw the moccasin track. Instantly his memory shuttled back to the moccasin track over the boot tracks that he had seen under the jackpine at Chevron. The full significance came immediately: Wallace had help.

Minutes later he saw where Ives had lined out with the two horses, heading into the desert, following the cattle sign, and he knew they were discovered. Patiently he searched for tracks returning, and when he did not find any he judged that whoever it was still remained on the desert.

Arnie Chance regarded those tawny shimmering wastes with narrow attention now. It was senseless to follow him, for the slightest wind could cover the tracks and he would miss him. On the other hand, the man with the moccasins was almost sure to be short of water. Returning – if he did return – he would hit for the closest trail to the rim, which meant this trail. Chance would have liked to greet him with a dozen guns, but he couldn't afford to leave Seco camp to summon them.

No, he would camp here, and when the man in moccasins returned he would have a welcome for him. For Chance knew shrewdly that he and Gove were utterly safe as long as the cattle sign out in the desert was kept secret.

He spent most of that day picking a vantage spot halfway up the trail from the desert to the rim. After much search he found what he wanted — a deep pothole in the rock which overlooked the trail. Nothing, not even a pack rat, could pass below him without being seen. He brought all his water and his grub and rigged his ground sheet for shade against the beating sun. In daylight he would sleep, trusting to the sounds of a horse passing below to waken him. At night he'd keep careful watch.

He didn't know how long it would take for the man in moccasins to return, but time was not an element. And Arnie Chance was as patient as any man who has his life at stake.

Ives was barely in sight of the rim when the sun set. Tonight he could easily reach Martha Macy's, pick up a change of horses, and find Dave. There was an urgency upon him that he had never experienced before. The secret seemed to be gnawing inside him, and Ives found that odd. Memory couldn't recall a time when he'd been anxious to tell anybody anything, but Ives felt like shouting this to the empty desert.

It was around midnight when Ives came to the talus slope where the trail let onto the desert, and he surveyed it quietly. It was hardly accurate to say he didn't like the feel of it, but that was what it amounted to. For unless Chance and Gove were wholly convinced that Wallace was alone, they would have returned to Seco. And they would have seen his tracks down here, which were too numerous to hide. Ives would have liked to climb the rim by some other trail, but they were too far distant, and his water was too short.

He studied the dark wall, listening, hearing nothing, getting the feel of it, like some wary animal. His mare was restive and thirsty, but Ives checked her and waited. He didn't like this, yet he knew he was going through with it. But he might as well use sense about it.

He'd been leading the pack horse. Now he pulled him up, untied the rope, and gave him a cut across the rump with the knotted end of it.

The pack horse, sensing that he was nearer water than he'd been for days, moved with alacrity, mounting into the wedge of black that was the trial's beginning.

Ives slipped out of the saddle, ground-haltered his mare and silently followed the pack horse.

The canyon was steep-walled, and the trail climbed abruptly over the face of the rock. The shoes of the pack horse clattered loudly on the rock and echoed and reechoed between the walls as the horse scrambled for footing. It was so dark ahead that Ives could barely see the horse. He himself clung to the deepest shadow, moving with utter noiselessness, alert and listening.

When the rifle went off some ten feet over his head the whole night seemed to erupt in one shattering blast.

Ives's horse shrilled and went down, kicking viciously, madly, against the side of the canyon wall.

Ives froze against the wall, listening. Above him he heard a man's boots scuffing against rock, then the sound died away.

Ives had a choice now, and he didn't hesitate. Swiftly he ran up the trail, deeper into the gloom, making no sound at all. When he heard the sound of a man running toward him down the trail he pulled into the deep shadow and flattened himself against the wall.

He could hear the runner panting now, his boots pounding the rock floor. Ives stood utterly motionless. The man passed him on the dead run, passed so close Ives could have reached out and touched him. But Ives didn't move. There would be time to settle his score when so much didn't depend on his getting to Dave.

When the running figure was past, Ives turned and noiselessly climbed the trail. He moved swiftly, expertly, his moccasins whispering on the rock.

Where the walls broke away for the mouth of the arroyo Ives climbed over the last tongue of rock that flanked the brush fence and then paused, listening intently.

Soon he heard it — the restless snort of a horse staked out under the closest cedar.

Ives went over to him. The horse was saddled and bridled, for this man wasn't the kind to cut off all retreat. It was Arnie Chance's horse, Ives saw.

Ives mounted him and headed him toward Martha Macy's not even bothering to hide his tracks. For Chance, he knew, would have four precious hours till daylight, and he would spend them getting to Gove as fast as Ives's jaded mare could take him.

CHAPTER 18

Dave hadn't been at the appointed meeting place last night, and Ives hadn't shown up. These two facts had young Pete Framm half wild from worry. He'd hung around Hilliard all day, and as each rider drifted into town for a bite to eat or a change of horses Pete would scan his face for the sign of elation that would indicate Dave had been cornered or captured. And each time, seeing nothing except a harried weariness, Pete felt as if he'd been given a fresh reprieve, until, past midday, his hopes began to rise again. It didn't seem possible, but it had been six days since Dave had broken out of Hilliard, and he was still free.

Sheriff Kinsley rode in in late afternoon, looking baffled and saddle-weary and quietly raging. To the men on the street who called to him Kinsley paid no attention, did not even notice them.

Pete smiled with a quiet elation when he saw it and held his patience until dark.

At dusk he rode out of town, picked up the

horse he'd hobbled in the timber above town, and then circled around to the camp where Dave and Ives had first met. There was a lot Pete had to tell Dave, the most important, of course, being Beth's message she'd given him.

Pete pulled into the camp, dismounted, and unpacked the cooked grub he'd had cached out with the horse. He didn't build a fire but sat there in the dark, smoking endless cigarettes, listening until he could hear his own blood pounding through his veins.

After two hours it came, the thin, true whistle from out in the night.

Pete came to his feet, answering, and presently Dave rode into the camp.

"Man, man," Pete said, walking up to his horse. "You all right?"

"I've grown to this saddle," Dave said. His voice was husky, but Pete knew this was because he hadn't used it for two days.

Dave swung down with a grunt, and Pete said, "They been crowdin' you, Dave?"

"Pretty hard. Ives back yet?"

"Not yet," Pete said gloomily. "Come on and eat."

Wisely Pete refrained from telling his news until Dave had eaten. Dave knelt there in the dark, wolfing down the cold food. Having missed Pete last night, he had gone hungry all day, and now he ate with a savage hunger.

Finished, he put his back against a tree and rolled his smoke. When he struck his match and cupped it in his palms Pete had a look at him. Dave's face told the whole story of these past few days. A black beard stubble blurred the sharp planes of his face but could not hide the gaunted cheeks or his sunken eyes. Salt dried sweat faintly crusted his thick eyebrows. His big hand shook as he held the match.

"What happened last night?" Pete asked.

"They had me cornered in a canyon of the Little Dun and didn't know it," Dave said. "I sat there in water up to my neck for five hours until they'd rolled in."

Pete said, "What do you reckon has happened to Ives?"

"Nothing."

"Get ready for a jolt," Pete said.

"What is it?"

"Beth Hilliard stopped me in town yesterday afternoon. She told me to tell Martha to tell you that she's sellin' Chevron to Hyam."

Dave sat up, yanking the cigarette from his lips. "Has she sold?" he asked swiftly.

"No. She said she'd wait on word from you."

"Ah." Dave sank back against the tree. "Hyam," he said musingly, reflectively, and was silent.

"It don't add up," Pete said. "What does that

tinhorn want with Chevron?"

"I dunno," Dave said wearily. "My first guess is he figures it's a gamble. He saw me take a chance reaching Beth to see if she'd still sell the place, so he figures I want it bad. And if I want it bad enough I'll pay his price for it."

Pete swore softly. "Has Buckley got the money to up his ante?"

"No."

Pete said quietly, "Then let me take care of him, Dave."

"Wait," Dave said.

Pete was silent, barely checking his impatience. It would be a pleasure to hand out such a beating to Hyam that he'd leave the country. Pete, remembering his first conversation with Hyam, relished the thought. He had taken one of those unreasoning instantaneous dislikes to Hyam on first sight, and the thought of the man was enough to prod his anger.

Dave spoke quietly now, feeling his way. "Forget all that, Pete. Hyam may be an answer to all this."

"How's that?"

"Ives and Buckley don't want Chevron. All they want is to keep Gove from getting it. Maybe Ives will say to let Hyam buy it. That's good money for Beth."

Pete said slowly, "I never thought of that."

"But he doesn't buy before Ives comes back.

That's what we got to stop. What if they corner me tomorrow? When Beth hears it she'll sell to Hyam."

"You got a package then," Pete conceded dryly. "You can't scare him off and you can't let him on."

"I reckon I can," Dave murmured. "I can keep him till Ives knows about it."

"Take him with you?" Pete asked unbelievingly. "Even you can't crowd your luck that far, Dave."

"Con has got a room above his saloon."

Pete was silent, waiting.

"You better ride in and ask him if we can use it."

"Use it how?" Pete asked blankly.

"We can't chase him off, and with all these riders swarming this country, we couldn't hide him. All right, let's hide him under Kinsley's nose. Take him and hold him above Con's saloon until Ives gets back."

The gall of the thing held Pete silent. And then he grinned into the night. It was wild and it was risky, but it made Dave Wallace's kind of sense, and he liked it.

He stood up. "This is my job."

"It's both our jobs," Dave corrected him. "Hyam will fight, and this has got to be quiet. You ride in and ask Con. I'll drift in and meet you under the bridge."

Pete shook his head in the dark, speechless for once. Wallace had been hounded through these hills by fifty men, had gone sleepless and hungry, and yet he was going into Hilliard tonight. Pete said quietly, "Well, I'm damned," and walked over to his horse.

When Pete was gone Dave got to his feet. Otherwise he would have slept there, with the cigarette in his lips. He moved restlessly around the camp and he wondered somberly where Ives was. He wished he felt as confident as he had let on to Pete. Six days and no sign of the old wolfer. If Chance had caught him there at Seco camp and suspected him, then Ives was dead. And if he was dead, then Dave had played out his hand, because he couldn't keep this up. No sleep, a jaded horse, the necessity of keeping on the move all the time, the chances he took that increased daily — one of these would trap him in the end. His luck was wearing thin; he felt it, as a man feels a premonition of catastrophe.

There would be Pete left, of course, but a few more days of this and Pete couldn't help him, for Kinsley would wonder at the change of horses and trace down the source of the fresh supply. That left fat Con Buckley, who was powerless to help, a prisoner of his own flesh. It was Buckley who had put up the money to buy Chevron, but even now, when Dave was in

278

doubt, he did not think of asking Buckley about Hyam. No, he needed Ives, had to have him, and Ives wasn't here.

Dave judged he'd allowed Pete enough of a head-start, and he saddled his fresh horse, mounted, and headed again toward Hilliard. There was a heaviness of spirit upon him that he couldn't shake. What they had planned tonight was a last desperate measure, and he knew Hyam could be hidden for only a few hours, or days at the most. After that if Ives didn't return, or returned from the Seco camp with nothing that would help them, then Dave knew they were finished. True, Beth Hilliard would have received a fair price for Chevron, but Gove and Chance, who had lied and framed and murdered, came off free, while he was hunted out of the country. He wondered bitterly if his words to Beth the other night had been believed and he doubted it. She was loyal to Gove, and nothing short of clumsy blunder on Gove's part would change her.

He circled above Hilliard and paused on the lip of the canyon, looking down upon the town. It seemed deserted, although there were lights in the hotel, store, and saloon. But the tie rails were empty. He had succeeded in pulling most of the posse away from town to the north in the last three days.

He left his horse in the timber and afoot took

to the wagon road above town. When he came to the bridge he paused and looked at the hotel. Lamps were lighted in the lobby, but there seemed to be nobody around. Had Hyam joined the posse?

Dave slipped down the bank and hunkered down beneath the bridge, waiting for Pete. He put his head on his folded arms and was immediately asleep.

He roused when Pete shook him by the shoulder.

"Con's not there," Pete murmured.

"Hyam in town?"

"I didn't want to ask the barkeep."

Dave rose wearily, "The street clear?"

"The whole town is, far as I can make out."

Dave was silent a moment, then asked, "Sure Con wasn't upstairs?"

"The barkeep said no." He peered in the darkness at Dave. "You want to risk it?"

"We got to," Dave said. "You go and look for Hyam. I'll move up to the veranda to the south of the door. Toll him out with his back to me. I'll rap him over the head, then you hand him over the railing to me, and I'll follow the river back to Con's."

Pete nodded and climbed the bank, Dave behind him. Pete went ahead up the steps. When Dave reached the top step he saw Pete haul up in the doorway, then turn, look back, and tilt his head toward the lobby. Softly Dave moved up against the wall, and when he was set Pete went on.

Dave heard Pete say, "Hyam," twice, and then there was a blurred, answering grunt. Hyam, Dave judged, had been roused from a nap in one of the lobby chairs.

Pete said, "Miss Hilliard's down at Rollins'. She'd like to see you."

There was a pause, and then Hyam said in a skeptical voice, "Miss Hilliard left town a half-hour ago."

"That's funny," Pete drawled, "because she's at Rollins' now."

"Have her come up."

Pete's voice took on an edge. "There's nothin' I'd rather do than kick you down there, Hyam. You want me to?"

A chair creaked, and then Hyam drawled, "You couldn't do it, but it won't be necessary to try."

Dave drew his gun, looked swiftly down the street, saw nobody, and then hugged the wall.

Pete and Hyam stepped through the door almost together, Hyam a little ahead of Pete. As he stepped onto the veranda Hyam turned his head. He caught the motion of Dave's downswinging arm, dodged back into Pete, and yelled wildly, "Wallace! Here's Wallace!"

Pete whipped an arm around his neck, choking off his cries, and Dave clipped him savagely in the jaw with his fist. Hyam sagged in Pete's arms, and Dave knelt down, saying swiftly, "Put him across my back."

Upstairs they heard the sound of tramping feet.

Dave rose, Hyam across his shoulders, and said, "Hit for under the bridge, Pete! Move!"

Pete lunged past him and down the steps. Dave was half-way down them when a window in the second story above the veranda slammed open and a man bawled, "There he is!" And a gun went off.

Pete Framm paused, streaked up his gun, and sent a shot at the window. The answering shot boomed into the plank walk. Somebody was lunging down the steps inside, taking them three at a time.

Dave knew instantly that this was it. They couldn't hide under the bridge, nor could he reach his horse.

He yelled, "Light out, Pete. I'll catch up with you!"

Pete ran toward him now, saying, "Drop him, Dave, and get your horse!"

Dave only shook his head, running across the street for the closest darkness. The sharpshooter in the window upstairs bawled, "He's cutting across the road!"

A second man opened fire from the hotel doorway.

And then the barkeep from the Olympus, sawed-off shotgun in his hand, slammed through the door of the Olympus. He saw Dave, Hyam still on his shoulder, running across the street. He whipped up his shotgun and let go with one barrel. The range was long, but the shot still had enough power to sting savagely as it pelted Dave's side.

He was on the far walk now, Pete behind him and two men were now shooting from the hotel. A third had covered the bridge.

Pete drove the man in the back door into the lobby and said with rising excitement, "What's the word, Dave?"

The bartender let go again, and the shot raked along the front of the warehouse. Another puncher, shooting on the run, piled down the boardwalk toward them, and the man on the bridge opened up.

Dave knew this was the finish. He said, "Cut down the river, Pete, and take a chance. So long!"

He approached the door of the warehouse, kicked it savagely, and when it swung on its creaking hinges he lunged in. His foot went through the rotting floor, and he crashed on his face, Hyam sailing over his head. Pete lunged in behind him, kicked the door shut, then ran to the boarded-up window. Raising his foot, he kicked a pair of boards loose, poked his gun through, and emptied it at the hotel.

The answering shots boomed into the clapboards of the warehouse.

Dave said harshly, "Pete, clear out of here! Get out while you can!"

"No chance," Pete said comfortably. Dave could hear him loading his gun.

Dave found Hyam, dragged him across the floor and rolled him against the front of the building, then knelt by Pete, breathing hard.

"Listen, kid," he said swiftly, "you've still got a chance in the river. Take it, but hurry up!"

"I'm stickin'," Pete said.

"Damn you, you don't see it!" Dave said angrily. "This is it!"

"Sure it is. I bought in, didn't I?"

Then Dave heard a voice lift into the night, calling: "You back there in the river, Monty?" It was the voice of Decker, the old jailer.

And from the back of the warehouse there came the answer. "We got two men back here, Al."

Dave moved over to Hyam and lifted the gambler's gun. He was still unconscious from the savage blow on the jaw.

Dave stood up then, against the wall, and said quietly, "Well, kid, we're in for some fun."

"You figure to stand 'em off, Dave?"

"Until they'll trade us horses for Hyam," Dave said grimly. "Save your shells, kid, and keep away from the window."

The blast of a dozen guns blanketed his last words. When they had eased off Pete yelled tauntingly, "Come on over, boys."

Oddly enough Dave smiled in the darkness. This was the end, maybe, but it was a relief to know it.

That evening at eight Beth had left Jess in the hotel lobby, saying that she would go and get some sleep before she rode out to see Dave and asked him to call her at ten-thirty that evening.

She went to her room, changed to denim pants and shirt, turned out the lamp, and listened. Presently a half-dozen men came up the stairs. They were walking softly, and she knew Jess had warned them to go quietly because she was sleeping. When they were past, she opened her door and saw the last man, Jess Gove, filing into Hyam's room. Presently the sound of cards being shuffled and the click of chips came to her, and she knew a poker game had started.

She slipped out of her room and downstairs then. Hyam was dozing in his chair. She crossed the lobby without waking him, descended the steps, and walked down the almost deserted street.

At the stable she got her horse, climbed the grade, then circled town and finally picked up the wagon road to Chevron.

She rode slowly, figuring there was plenty of time to make the second ford by ten. She was nervous, however, made so by an unnameable excitement. Now that the test was here she shrank from going through with it. Since she had written that note and showed it to Jess she had changed her mind almost hourly about Jess Gove. Today she would have given anything to have it settled, but now that the time approached she wished it could be put off. But there was the memory of Dave Wallace's words and the knowledge that she would never know peace until the truth or falseness of them was proven.

When she came to the third ford she was suddenly in a desperate hurry. The second ford lay two miles above. That was the distance that separated her from knowing.

Now she began to pick out the landmarks as best she could on this black night. She couldn't see a yard ahead of her, for the overhang of the pines even blotted out the starlight.

But coming to the switchback that let onto Second Ford, she was calm enough. She didn't know what she'd expected to find, but there was nothing ahead of her. The murmur of the Little Dun as it rushed across the gravel ahead of her came plainly through the night.

And then she felt an odd mixture of relief and disappointment. It was relief that Jess had kept his word and disappointment that Dave, who could be so right, was so terribly wrong now.

Her horse stepped into the water now, splashing it.

And in that moment the night came alive.

"Stay where you are, Wallace, or you're a dead man!"

It was Sam Kinsley's bull voice shouting. And then a kerosene-soaked bundle of rags sailed into the road behind her, and by its light she saw a half-dozen men, rifles leveled at her, across the river. Behind her there were another half dozen. And from the brush beside the bank Sam Kinsley kneed his horse into the Little Dun, raining the water in flashing curtains as he came.

Sam was a dozen feet from her when he recognized her. He reined his horse in so violently, it reared, then settled back.

"Beth!" Sam said stupidly. He had a six-gun in his fist.

"I'm a little early," Beth said quietly.

Sam came up to her now, his jaw set ominously. There was pale rage in his face as he pulled up alongside her, forgetting to holster his gun.

"You might have been shot!"

"It didn't work, did it, Sam?" Beth said quietly. "Jess told you, didn't he?"

"I don't know what Jess has to do with this," Sam said flatly, angrily.

"You're a clumsy liar, Sam — almost as clumsy a liar as you are a sheriff." She paused, unafraid of the ominous look in Kinsley's face. "Jess lied to me, like he's lied to all of you. You see, I forged that note to myself, Sam. I did it to see if Jess Gove wanted Wallace trapped and jailed or killed. And I've found out."

"He tried to help us!" Sam blurted out in sullen anger.

"You poor fool!" Beth said bitingly. "Gove is the man who's framed Wallace from the very start!"

She was interrupted by a man calling, "Kinsley, somebody's comin'."

They all looked down the road, some of the men running ahead, in case it might be Wallace. But this rider was coming at a dead gallop, and when he saw the rags burning in the road, surrounded by the possemen, he yelled exultantly.

When he rode up into the circle of firelight there was a wild excitement in his face. He reined his horse in, saw Kinsley, and said, "We got your man cornered, Sheriff. Wallace is in the warehouse next to the Olympus, and we got fifteen guns on him!"

CHAPTER 19

Hilliard was bedlam. A dozen rifles from as many different positions kept pouring slugs into the old warehouse. Beth could hear them long before she saw the town. The ride back was a mad scramble, in which Beth held her own among the possemen. Their guide told them to avoid the bridge road, which was under the fire of Wallace's guns, so they circled the town and came down the grade to Rollins' store, which was just out of the line of fire.

Beth reined up at the same time Sam did. The guide said, "Decker's at the hotel. Better circle in back of the buildings."

Beth looked downstreet where the rifle fire was racketing, put spurs to her horse, and started down it.

"Beth!" Sam roared.

He raced after her and caught the bridle of her horse and hauled him up.

"Get down!" Sam said angrily.

"Get out of the way, Sam!"

"I order you into Rollins' store as sheriff!"

"While you butcher an innocent man! I won't go! Let go that bridle, Sam, or I'll ride you down!"

"You fool, can't you see Wallace has got the whole town driven to cover! He'll shoot you!"

Beth only smiled pityingly and roweled her horse. He reared and pawed out with his front feet, and Sam had to let go the bridle. Beth calmly rode down the middle of the street. Two men forted up in the barbershop called to her to go back, but she went on. The shooting from the warehouse ceased, and Beth put her horse over to it and reined up by the window whose frame was chewed to splinters by rifle fire.

"Dave," she called.

"Here, Beth." Dave's voice came from just inside the window.

"You were right about Jess, Dave," Beth said quietly. "He's a liar. I don't know what else he is, but I will know. I'm going to stop this, Dave, if it takes all week. And this time Jess Gove won't get in my way."

When he didn't answer Beth said, "Are you listening, Dave?"

"I heard," Dave said quietly.

"Don't let them take you," Beth said. "Whatever you do, don't let them take you until I can stop this."

Beth put her horse across the street now and dismounted at the tie rail in front of the hotel.

These men watched her in silence from the shelter of the hotel lobby as she mounted the steps, crossed the veranda, and stepped into the room.

Sam had cricled around in back of the buildings and come into the hotel through the rear entrance. He stood there by the men, his face dark with fury.

Beth looked these men over and saw Gove, a head taller than the rest, watching her.

And then she saw Ives. He was leaning idly against the wall, his eyes alert and questioning and friendly. Beth had a second of deep bitterness then when she looked at him. If Ives had only been here to help when she needed him. If he could only help her now in what she was going to do.

The rifle fire started up again.

Sam said angrily, "Beth you ought —"

She was paying no attention, and he stopped talking.

Beth walked toward the men, and their circle split and she was face to face with Jess Gove. She looked at Sam then and pointed to Jess and said, "There's the man you should be hunting — Jess Gove."

The unexpectedness of her declaration left these men speechless, staring at her and Gove.

Jess said mildly, reprovingly, "Beth, what are you saying?"

Beth looked at him angrily. "That was a forged note I showed you, Jess. It wasn't from Wallace. And you had Sam there to kill him."

Her face was pale, and her lips were trembling in spite of her effort at control, but her eyes were bright and angry and determined.

She looked at Kinsley and said coldly, "Would you be interested in knowing, Sam, that Tip Macy was really murdered? Gove denied it, and I denied it when you asked us, but it's true."

Kinsley looked searchingly at Beth and then shuttled his attention to Gove, a question in his face.

Gove said gently, "Beth, Beth. What will Sam think of us?" He looked at Kinsley and said quietly, "Yes, it's true. I didn't tell you and Beth didn't tell you, because Tip was rustling Chevron beef. We covered it up to save Martha Macy the humiliation of being branded as a rustler's wife."

"The same Martha Macy that left Chevron because her love affair with Pete Framm was discovered by you?" Beth asked bitingly.

Gove's face altered a little. "That's right."

"You're lying," Beth said flatly. "She left because she was afraid you and Arnie Chance would kill her!"

The accusation was like a whiplash popping in the still room. The occasional rifle blasting away outside did not seem to reach this stillness.

Kinsley stared stupidly at Beth, and Beth went on, talking to Kinsley: "All this trouble with Wallace has come about because Dave knew Tip Macy didn't die in a blizzard, Sam. And Gove has tried to kill him or drive him out of the country — because he feared Wallace would learn the truth."

"You got that from Wallace?" Sam asked thinly.

"I did."

Kinsley snorted in angry contempt. "You're a headstrong girl, Beth. Don't turn into a busybody woman. Let us handle this. Go to bed."

Beth looked despairingly around her, and her glance settled on Ives. He was watching her quietly, gravely. And then Beth saw it plainly: He winked solemnly.

She turned on Kinsley. "But, Sam, don't you see how it works out! Don't you —?"

"Beth, go to bed!" Kinsley said flatly, harshly.

He strode the two steps toward her and took her arm firmly and said angrily, "You're beside yourself. You don't know what you're saying. Go upstairs and lie down and let us take care of this!"

Beth tried to shake his arm off, but he held her firmly. Desperately she looked around at these men, at Ives.

"Don't any of you believe me?" she cried.

And Ives again winked.

Sam moved her implacably toward the stairs. There was a movement, a murmur among the men, and then two of them moved, and Arnie Chance, dusty and sweating, stepped into the circle of men and came up to Gove.

Beth heard him say quietly, "Rollins wants to see you, Jess."

Beth, her foot on the bottom step, looked bleakly at Chance, and then she saw Ives push away from the wall.

He walked swiftly and silently up to Gove, raised an arm, and slashed him across the face with the back of his hand.

Then turning, he said to Kinsley, "I can talk now because Chance is here." He paused. "Gove is a murderer. He's a rustler, too, and I got proof that will hang him and Chance both!"

Arnie Chance had just arrived from Seco, and he had sized up the situation immediately. He knew he must get Gove away. And when Ives spoke out something clicked in Arnie's mind. He remembered how soundlessly Ives had approached Gove and he looked at Ives's feet. Here was the man with moccasins.

What happened then came with the speed of lightning.

Chance was standing near the window. He raised his foot, kicked out the sash, and dived out the window.

Ives made a grab for him, missed, and yelled, "Cut him off!"

But these men here were still too bewildered to act.

Chance hit the ground on all fours, came to his feet, running toward the street. He saw the horse Beth had left at the tie rail.

He ducked under the rail, vaulted in the saddle, and roweled the horse savagely toward the bridge and the grade.

Dave Wallace, watching at the window, saw Chance duck under the tie rail, and he knew instantly that this had broken.

He ran for the door, tripping again on the hole in the rotten floor. He reached the door, yanked it open, and ran out into the dark street.

Chance was leaned over the neck of his horse, which was already on the bridge. Someone on the hotel veranda was shouting.

Dave lifted his gun, let it settle, and fired.

Chance's horse missed stride, and then his front legs buckled and he went down with a crash that boomed heavily on the bridge.

Chance went kiting over his head, landing on all fours and skidding on his face. He rolled over twice, came to his knees. In the half-light that reached the bridge Dave saw him come to his feet, his hand streaking for his gun.

Dave stopped and thumbed back the hammer of his gun and lifted it.

Chance shot from the hip, shot wildly, and the slug kicked up a geyser of dust at Dave's feet. Dave's hand steadied, and he brought Chance into the dim notch of his sight, and again Chance shot, and Dave heard the slug whisper past him, and then Dave, firing for Chance's gun flash, squeezed the trigger.

Chance stepped back, a full bracing step, and now Dave walked toward him, shooting carefully, implacably. Chance backed to the bridge rail, shot again, and then Dave halted and took careful aim.

But before he could fire again Chance had arched slowly backward over the rail of the bridge. Dave heard him hit the shallow water of the Little Dun, heard the water splash back again.

Kinsley saw all this from the porch, a baffled rage welling up inside him. When Chance went over the bridge rail the sight of him moved Kinsley into action. All he could see, all he knew was that Dave Wallace, the man he'd been hunting until he was half crazed with the doing of it, was standing there in the street alone.

He pulled his gun and raised it, and then he heard Beth's cry of protest, and he cocked his gun.

And then Beth brought both hands down on his gun arm just as he shot. The slug boomed into the porch steps, and wildly Sam brushed Beth aside with his arm and started to raise his gun again.

And then something fell across his shoulders, pinning his arms back with an iron strength.

It was Con Buckley's voice that spoke in his ear. "Drop that gun, you jug head! Drop it!"

Beth ran down the steps then and toward Dave. When she saw him standing there in the street, uncertain, waiting, but unhurt, she was so weak with relief that she couldn't speak for a moment.

"Are you hurt, Dave? Are you hurt?"

"Steady," Dave said gently. He put a hand out and took hers. He smiled then and looked beyond her to the veranda, at the men whose guns covered him.

"We got to finish this," he murmured.

He turned and called, "Come on, Pete. Bring Hyam."

They went up the steps to the veranda, where Kinsley, with Con's gun in his side, waited. There was a crazed look in Kinsley's face, as if the man had been pushed beyond human endurance.

Dave walked past him into the lobby, where Ives had a gun in Gove's back. At sight of Ives,

Dave sighed gently. "It's all right," he said to Beth.

The room was utterly still now, every man in it watching Dave.

Dave said quietly, bitterly, "Gove, I hope they hang you. Old as you are, I hope you hang."

Kinsley came up behind Dave now, walked past him, and faced Ives and Gove.

"Ives, you said Gove's a murderer and a cattle thief. In God's name, why did you say it!" His voice was tormented and bewildered.

Ives said sourly, "The evidence is out on the desert, Kinsley. All you got to do is look at it. Two thousand head of Chevron cattle — the steers Gove claimed were winterkilled — were drove across the desert."

Kinsley just stared at him as if he were insane and then looked blankly at the men around him. "Drove across the desert?" he echoed.

"That's right," Ives snarled. "The runoff of them blizzards all winter reached deep into the desert. Thirty miles out there in that damn sand there was a lake of the runoff. It held long enough to grow weeds around it. And Gove, under the cover of them dozen storms, moved his cattle across the Vermillion. He had water at this lake, the next water at the Bunchgrass Tanks, which was full then, and the next water at the Mesquite Hills."

There was complete silence now. Dave said quietly into it, "Then that's how Ed Seegrist got across the desert without water."

"He got the last of it," Ives said.

"Wait! Wait!" Kinsley said in angry vehemence. "Ives, where's proof?"

"There's old cattle sign for any man to see," Ives said truculently. "It heads from Seco camp straight out to this dry lake and beyond!"

Kinsley was mute. These men were looking at Gove now, who was watching Kinsley with a searching gaze.

"I don't believe it!" Kinsley shouted angrily. "How could he sell them once he got them across? He couldn't! You're framing Gove!"

A new voice said quietly, "No, he isn't. And I can tell you how Gove got rid of them."

Kinsley wheeled ponderously to see Tom Hyam step through the circle of listening men. "This is all I was waiting for," Hyam said. "This is all I needed." He reached in his coat and brought out his wallet and handed it to Kinsley. "It's hard to believe, Sheriff, but I'm a cattle inspector from across the line. That Chevron herd was reported to us purely by accident. A couple of the steers died in the drive to the railroad up north. A hand over on the Bullseye skinned one out and saw where the brand had been altered from Chevron to

Pine Tree. The shippers were paid, and they'd broken up and drifted out of the country. And I came into this country to check with Chevron."

He looked at Gove. "You don't know that, Gove, because you weren't at Chevron. But Chance was, and I knew Chance. His picture is pretty well known on the reward dodgers in our country. I left then, smelling something, and came back into this country as a tinhorn gambler and set up here. And I got enough to hang Gove, but no proof."

Beth said miserably, "What was it?"

Hyam looked over at Gove and smiled thinly. "Why, I saw Chance shoot Seegrist's horse that day. I told Gove I did. And Gove promised to split Chevron with me if I'd act as a dummy buyer to freeze you out, Wallace. He promised it at the very moment when Seegrist was shot by Chance."

Beth looked at Gove then, and the man she had known was gone. His face was still benign and kindly, even in this, and on it was an expression of amused tolerance. The old Gove, though, was vanished, because he had lived only in her mind and in the imagination of others.

Hyam said dryly, "Of course, once I'd bought Chevron he would have killed me, like Chance killed Seegrist."

"And like he killed Macy," Ives said sourly.

"Macy was suspicious, too. Kinsley, if you want proof of that, ask Martha Macy. She's at Rollins' store now. Macy showed up at Seco wash on the day of a drive, and they murdered him."

Kinsley was mute, his face anguished.

"The gang Gove split with across the line drove the beef across the desert," Hyam said. He reached for his billfold, taking it from Kinsley's lifeless hand, and pocketed it and turned to Dave.

"You had my plan shot to hell tonight, Wallace. I was waiting for Gove to give me the money, and then I'd turn him up with the proof." He smiled faintly. "You're a stubborn man, mister."

Kinsley looked at Gove now and said slowly, "Jess, you got anything to say?"

Gove simply looked at Beth and said, "Nothing at all."

Young Pete Framm said thinly, "When you're tried, Gove, Martha Macy will be sittin' in the front row in the courtroom. I want you to remember that."

He turned and walked out now, heading for Rollins' store and Martha. It was the signal for the other men to start talking. Kinsley, sensing the course their talk would take, took Gove upstairs away from them. Jess walked proudly, a head taller than these men. On the fifth step up the stairs he paused and looked down at the men watching. His glance settled on Beth, and she saw tears in his eyes.

She turned away, sick at heart, and Ives guided her into the dining room, which was empty. When she looked up Dave and Con Buckley were standing behind Ives.

"You thought I run out on you, didn't you, Beth?" Ives said gently.

Beth took his hand and squeezed it. "I – I guess I did, Ives. You didn't come."

Con Buckley said, "Ives was tearing up the country to help you, Beth. He couldn't do it in the open."

Ives said, "It was Con's money that Dave used to buy Chevron."

Beth bit her lip, nodding, acknowledging all this. Then she said suddenly, "Ives, what made Jess do it? Why did he do it to me?"

Ives smiled wryly, and there was the old cantankerous light in his eyes. "He was just so damn sick of being sweet and kind and nice, I think."

Beth smiled then in spite of herself, and somebody called Ives into the lobby. Con followed him, leaving Dave standing there, watching her.

She came up to him and stood before him, and she knew she was going to ask him the thing she had been wanting to know.

"Dave, do you remember what you said in

my room that night before Sam broke in? You said someday, when this was over, you'd tell me why you were doing it and how."

Dave nodded. "It was a deal I made with Ives. He promised to find Tip's killer if I would help you. And I didn't want to."

Beth was silent. She watched Dave searching for words, was afraid to speak, to help him.

"I didn't want to help until you came into jail that day and told me you didn't think I'd shot at Seegrist. I knew that there was nothing wrong with you, except you were too loyal. I had to help you then, because — well, I reckon I wanted to, Beth."

Someone stepped into the room, and they both looked up. It was Kinsley. He was utterly beaten, tired and baffled and bone-weary, and there was a somberness in his eyes that was not pleasant to see.

"I'm saying good-by, Beth," he said. "Decker will take care of Gove and the trial."

"Good-by?" Beth was genuinely bewildered. "You mean you're leaving the country, Sam?"

Kinsley nodded bleakly. "I'm drifting to a place where I can start over." He looked soberly at Dave and then back to Beth. "You remember, Beth, what I told you once? I said I'd never let you marry any man but me? I said I'd kill him first. All right, Beth, I've got eyes in my head. That's why I'm going — so I won't be hanged for murder."

Beth was mute. Kinsley put out his hand, and Beth took it. And then Kinsley turned to Dave.

"I don't like you," he said doggedly, with no heat. "Just remember this. If you don't make Beth happy I'll come back and kill you."

He wheeled and tramped out of the room then. Dave looked at Beth, and her face was flushed with shame.

Dave reached out and tilted up her chin. "He said all I have to say, Beth. And if I can't make you happy I hope he comes back."

Beth came to him then and couldn't speak in his arms.

THORNDIKE-MAGNA hopes you have enjoyed this Large Print book. All our Large Print titles are designed for easy reading, and all our books are made to last. Other Thorndike Press or Magna Print books are available at your library, through selected bookstores, or directly from the publishers. For more information about current and upcoming titles, please call or mail your name and address to:

THORNDIKE PRESS
P.O. Box 159
Thorndike, Maine 04986
(800) 223-6121
(207) 948-2962 (in Maine and Canada call collect)

or in the United Kingdom:

MAGNA PRINT BOOKS
Long Preston, Near Skipton
North Yorkshire,
England BD23 4ND
(07294) 225

There is no obligation, of course.